Reviews

Blood Curse - Loved it and can't wait to read more from you. Way to go girl!!!!!!!!!!! – *Jenn Kelloway*

Blood Curse - For a new author this book is a really good read. I couldn't put it down. I really hope there is a sequel because I need to know what happens to these cool characters. – **avongirl1331**

Blood Curse - <u>Ready for More</u> - This is not my typical genre for reading, but it certainly had me hooked from the beginning. Once I started I found it hard to put down. It left me wanting more. I am hooked and anxiously awaiting the next book. Great job Lynn. – *Bethany Mawbey*

Blood Curse - <u>Awsome read</u> -- This book was a really good read. I loved the characters. Once I started I couldn't put it down and it left me wanting more. I will be watching for the next book for sure. – *Debbie Henry*

Blood Connection - I thought the book was wonderful. I enjoyed it very much and can hardly wait to keep reading the rest of the series. Keep on writing and we will keep on reading. –*Marion Henderson*

Blood Curse

Lynn Marie Simpson

ISBN: 978-1-926898-28-5

Pine Lake Books
Canada
www.pinelakebooks.ca

DEDICATION

I dedicate this story to Don, who is now, and who will always be, the Keeper of my Heart.

ACKNOWLEDGMENTS

I would like to thank my sisters Debbie, Susie, Jean, and June, as well as my good friend Maggie. They not only read everything I write, but their input has helped to keep me on the right track. I also want to thank my children, Christopher and Dawn Marie, for reminding me that a person can do whatever they want, all they have to do is try.

Chapter One

The silence was deafening.

No insects. No wind in the leaves. Not the whisper of wings in the night. Nothing.

An owl hooted.

His vacant eyes turned towards the sound, and searched the treetops. Black, soulless eyes clashed with bright yellow ones. "Find your own dinner. This one's mine." He dismissed the owl as of no consequence.

He was young by vampire standards. At nearly a century old, he couldn't remember much about his previous life. He did not care to remember. His life was now. Anything before didn't matter.

For years, he had survived off the blood of animals. Mostly goats. How he hated goat blood. When the rumours of The Chupacabra first began, he had been insulted. Goatsucker! How dare they? Then he had felt their shock, and fear. It was intoxicating. It fed him. It made him powerful. Invincible.

He fed their fear in order to feed his own growing strength. Shape shifting into a half-man, half-beast, he would allow them glimpses of him as he fed on their livestock. All calculated to instil fear deep into their souls.

Soon, even that was not enough.

Then, early one evening he woke to the sounds of music, and laughing. Curiosity drew him. He approached a neighbouring farm to discover a dozen or so humans having a party. He could not believe the audacity. To be outside after the sun went down. Unafraid. This was his domain. He ruled the night. He had to do something. He did not dare lose his hold on these people. He truly believed he would die without their fear to feed him. He drew on their nightmares, and began to change.

His body shrunk until he stood about four feet tall. His eyes narrowed, grew longer, and glowed red. Fur and feathers sprouted in patches out of his gray skin. At the end of his short arms burst large, powerful claws, and a row of sharp spikes ran down his back and on top of his head. His legs, short and muscular, narrowed at the bottom, ending in three, clawed toes.

Boldly he approached the partiers. A woman spotted him. Her scream filled the night. It was music to his ears. Chaos ensued. Screaming. Shoving. Pushing. Mothers and fathers reached for small children. The humans trampled each other in their haste to reach the safety of the house.

The vampire stood in the midst of the confusion, intoxicated by their panic; their fear.

An explosion rent the air. A flash of light blinded him. An unearthly scream ripped through the night when the slug slammed into his body, narrowly missing his heart. Black blood spewed from the hole. The ground sizzled and smoked where his blood landed. Plants withered and died. A woman screamed when some of his blood splattered on her face, eating away her skin. In a rage, he reached out one clawed arm, and dragged the screaming woman to him. With his other clawed hand, he twisted back her head, exposing her neck. Fangs exploded in his mouth. He sank them into her neck, and drank.

This was ambrosia.

Her warm, fear-enhanced blood swept through his body, feeding his tissues and organs. He felt himself growing stronger than ever before. His muscles worked to push the slug from his body, and the hole closed. He drained the last drop of blood, dropped the woman's lifeless body to the ground, and slowly licked every drop from his protruding fangs.

Never again would he lower himself to drink the blood of an animal.

The owl hooted again, and flew to another tree.

Two miles away, a dog's ears twitched. The dog stopped, stuck its nose in the air, and sniffed. He growled deep in his throat acknowledging the owl, and continued in the same direction. He had to move slowly, picking a path through the dense brush that his human companions could follow.

The owl settled in the tree, and watched the scene below.

The child lay on a flat rock, surrounded by trees - a sacrificial lamb. The vampire tenderly rearranged her clothing. He made her more comfortable.

He spoke one word. "Wake." His voice was velvet seduction.

The girl opened her eyes, and stared at the man. Her mind began to scream but no sound escaped her mouth. Fresh tears ran down her cheeks, and mingled with dried tears and dust. She began to sob silently. Her mind struggled to break free of the invisible chains that held it, and her body, prisoner.

The vampire ran his tongue along his teeth. His smile widened. His canines grew.

"Don't cry little one," he whispered. His voice was soft, compelling. The girl's sobs lessened, and then stopped completely. Still the child's mind screamed in terror. The vampire took a step towards her, then another. With each step closer, his canines grew longer. His tongue reached out, and touched the tip of one long tooth, licking the cloudy liquid that dripped from it. "It will only hurt for a moment. I promise." He crooned, his voice hypnotic.

The owl mentally blinked.

The child stared at the vampire in silence, unable to break free. Her eyes were two, unseeing saucers, in her small, pale face. She was staring at the vampire, but she wasn't seeing him. She could not have been more than five or six, but her mind was busy trying to find a way to break free of the vampire's thrall before it was too late.

It was too late for her father.

The memory of watching as the vampire forced her father to him, helpless as the monster fed on him until there was nothing left, had her silently screaming again. She had tried to call out to her father, to wake him from the vampire's spell, but her voice was silent. Her pleas never reached him. They were swallowed by something dark and dangerous. Something she had led to them.

Her whole world had gone black, and she awoke here. In this time and place.

The child never moved a muscle as the vampire reached out, and lovingly caressed her hair. Gently he pushed it back from her face. He tilted her neck slightly, and stared with hunger at the small pulse beating there. He could smell the blood coursing through her veins. The beating of her heart pounded in his ears. Her silent screams roared in his mind. He had been dreaming of this moment since he had first heard that quiet voice whispering across the wind searching for someone like herself. Her power had drawn him like a beacon in the night.

He leaned towards the small, pulsating vein. His mouth opened wider. His teeth dripped. Slowly his tongue traveled the length of the slender vein, savouring the taste of her fear.

The owl shrieked.

The vampire jumped back from the child. Instinctively he threw his arms up to protect his face. A razor-sharp beak tore hunks of flesh from his arm. He howled in rage. His body began to shimmer. Before he could shape-shift, the owl struck again. There was a blur of feathers and blood. His blood. The owl struck relentlessly, heedless of the foul blood that covered its feathers. It avoided the vampire's counter attacks with ease.

Suddenly, it stopped.

A snarl came from behind. The vampire spun around to face this new danger. He did not realize his mistake until it was too late.

A fully-grown wolf leapt at his exposed throat, clamping its teeth down in a vice-like grip. The two bodies hit the ground together. The vampire was frantic. Nothing had challenged him in his short life. He clawed viciously at the wolf. The wolf held tight, ignoring the blood trickling from the wounds on its side, and covering its white coat. It never loosened its grip on the vampire's throat.

The vampire's body went limp. Still the wolf kept its hold. Not until the vampire's head rolled back, nearly severed from its body, did the wolf loosen its hold. The wolf wasn't finished. It clamped its teeth in what was left of the vampire's throat, and chewed completely through.

The vampire's head rolled to the side of its body. Energy sizzled in the air. Then both head and body burst into a cloud of dust, and drifted harmlessly to the ground.

The wolf lay on the ground panting. Its body shimmered for a moment, and then changed.

Clad in a cotton shirt, blue jeans, and running shoes, Jade rose from the ground. She took a minute to listen to the familiar sounds of the jungle. The wind once again, whispered in the trees. A million insects began to buzz. A mouse scurried through the dried grass. The jungle had already begun to reclaim itself from the vile touch of the undead.

A rustle in the jungle about a half-mile away signalled the approach of the search party.

There were no silent screams. No silent pleas for help.

Jade slapped at a mosquito that thought she might provide its dinner, and limped over to the rock, one hand pressed against the wound in her side. The child lay on the stone alter, her eyes closed. If it were not for the slow, steady heartbeat, and the shallow breathing, Jade would think she had died.

Jade spoke softly, but the child didn't respond.

Tears swam in amber eyes, but Jade refused to allow them to escape.

"It's over honey," she whispered. "It's time to come back." She continued to talk soothingly to the child, as she gathered her into her arms and went to meet the search party.

It was time to go home.

Chapter Two

In another part of the jungle, a lone wolf snuffled at the body of what was once a very beautiful woman. Her translucent skin had been bitten and gnawed, having provided dinner for the very hungry jungle. Her body had been used and abused before her veins were drained completely of their life's precious fluid, and she had been discarded like yesterday's garbage.

The scent of the child was all over the woman; Strong and sweet beneath the clinging, vile scent of the vampire, the scent that had led Matthew to these grisly remains. The body of the man was two days old when they discovered it. This one was a day. If they did not find the child soon, chances were that she would be dead too.

Matthew puzzled over the strange behaviour of the vampire. It had never separated its victims before. Entire families drained and left together. Why then, had he not drained this family the same way? Never mind the fact that the vampire was traveling on foot making it easy, maybe a little too easy Matthew thought, to track him.

An owl hooted to the south. The wolf's ears twitched and his muzzle twisted into the semblance of a smile. That one small hoot carried with it a wealth of information. The vampire was about to draw its last breath, and the child lived.

The wolf growled at a vulture that dared land too near the body, and then in a slow, fluid motion the wolf began to shift until a muscular, dark-skinned man appeared beside the body. With a casual wave of his hand, the way Jade had taught him, he clothed himself in a snug shirt that showed his rippling muscles, skin tight jeans, and non-descript runners.

Matthew preferred his wolf form, and working with Jade allowed him the freedom to be one. As part of an elite search and rescue squad, nobody questioned the presence of a wolf. If anyone wondered where the wolf went when the man was present, they didn't mention it. Right now, the man was needed. The wolf could not carry the woman's body, and the man refused to leave her behind to feed the jungle.

With several rapid movements of his hands Matthew silently chanted a few words, and fashioned a sturdy sheet. With great care, treating the woman as if she were precious cargo, he gently wrapped her broken body. Then lifting her in his powerful arms, he carried her several miles through the jungle to the town where the body of her husband waited.

Chapter Three

The door flew open with a bang, and Gemma stumbled in. Laughing, she caught the edge of the door to keep herself steady. Her heart beat frantically, in tune to the music as the noise reverberated through her mind. A dime-sized medallion, with the head of a wolf etched in it, hung from a simple chain around her neck. Her hand moved automatically to the ancient piece of metal. It was warm and familiar against her skin as she gently rubbed it between her thumb and forefinger. The mindless movement calmed her.

Dio, what was she doing here? How had Sara managed to convince her that this was a good idea? She raked the long, slender fingers of one hand through her blonde bangs, and shoved them back. Their shortness was still a shock.

"You look fine." Sara gave her a small nudge, and they continued into the room. The door slammed behind them. "Don't worry. Nobody is going to ask for I.D. Not now. With that cut and color you look five years older." Dancing blue eyes scanned the room. "Just remember, if anyone asks your name is Caitlin. Oh look, there's an empty table over there." She pointed towards the far side of the crowded dance floor.

"I knew we should've come earlier. It's always packed this time of night."

Gemma peered across the room. How could Sara see anything? The room was so thick with cigarette smoke you would think they were running a fog machine. The wall lights placed strategically around the room were so dim they created more shadows than light. Overhead, lasers crisscrossed the dance floor, cutting through the fog like multi-coloured blades. It was eerie and disorienting, even with her enhanced sight.

"I'm not sure this is such a good idea." Gemma tugged her tight-fitting sweater down in an attempt to cover her bare midriff. When that didn't work, she tried to pull the waistband of her jeans higher.

Sara slapped at her hands. "Stop it. You don't want to draw attention to yourself, and besides you look great." She smiled, and waved at the bouncer who was eyeing them from the corner of the bar. The bouncer waved back then turned his attention to a couple of boys who were trying to get served.

"I told you they weren't going to bother us."

"Are you sure this top isn't too short?

"Yes. I'm sure." Sara shook her head, and let out an exaggerated sigh. Then she slipped her arm through Gemma's, and tugged her in the direction of the table. "Come on, Caitlin." She winked conspiratorially. "Quit fussing and move before someone else gets that table."

The hair on Gemma's arms bristled as a chill caressed her skin. Instantly on alert, she scanned the crowd for signs of danger. Nothing. She shrugged it off. Probably just a draft from the doorway mixed with her reluctance to be here. She gave one last, longing glance at the exit, and allowed Sara to lead her through the maze of scattered chairs and tables.

A couple of drinks on the table, and a sweater tossed casually on the back of a chair, staked a prior claim. "Damn!" Sara blurted. Quickly she covered her mouth, and glanced at

Gemma. Her blue eyes were dancing with humour. "Oops. Sorry."

Gemma rolled her eyes, otherwise ignoring the slip. She had known Sara for years, and the girl was incorrigible. "Looks like someone beat us to the table." Gemma found it difficult to hide her relief, while at the same time wishing she were even half as adventurous as Sara. "I guess we should call it a night and go home."

Movement from a table near the back exit caught their attention. Sara was quick; you had to give her that. Before Gemma could do a thing, Sara approached the man sitting alone.

"Hi." She batted her eyelashes at him, flirting outrageously. "I couldn't help noticing you all alone. You don't mind if my friend *Caitlin* and I join you?"

The man shrugged, and indicated the free chairs.

Gemma couldn't shake the feeling she was being stalked. It made her nervous. Every nerve in her body screamed for her to turn, and run while she still had the chance. Again, she searched the room, but found nothing she would call threatening.

Sara sat in the chair directly opposite the man. Gemma reluctantly pulled out a chair between the two, and followed suit. She wasn't completely at ease. She had the distinct impression they weren't wanted here.

"I'm David." He tipped his beer up, and drained the bottle. "Can I buy you girls a drink?"

"No," Gemma blurted. She closed her eyes, and mentally gave herself a swift kick in the butt. "Thanks." Great. She must really come across as some kind of idiot. All the guy did was offer to buy them a drink, and she practically chewed his head off. To make things worse, at this moment she wanted a drink more than anything in the world.

Sara winked at David. "Don't mind my friend here. She doesn't get out much." Sara looked around the room. "I need to use the ladies room anyway. I'll grab the drinks on the way back."

Sara rose from the table. She waved Gemma back down when she would have followed. "Wait here, Caitlin. I can handle it."

Gemma was nervous. She knew she was out of her depth. If she were the type that cursed, she would be cursing Sara right now. What was Sara thinking anyway, leaving her at the table alone? Okay. Strictly speaking, she wasn't alone, and that, in itself, was the problem. Left to her own devices she would probably make an even bigger fool of herself than she already had.

Gemma felt eyes boring into the back of her head. She turned quickly, hoping to catch whoever it was, and found herself staring into electric pools of blue. Her breath caught in her throat. She was drowning. She couldn't tear her eyes from his. The air crackled with tension. The noise in the bar began to dim. The sound of her own breathing roared in her ears.

"Hey you two, look what I found at the bar."

The spell was shattered. Gemma turned to Sara letting her breath out in a rush.

Sara set a tray on the table, and began setting beers around. "This is Mark." Sara flashed a grin at the man standing behind her. "He was just hanging around the bar all by himself so I took pity on him and asked him to join us."

Gemma would have had to tilt her head back even if she were standing. "Hi." My god he was tall.

Mark bobbed his head in her direction. "Hi. You must be Caitlin. Sara's been telling me all about you." He winked, took a swig of beer, and turned to David. "You must be David? I hope you don't mind me crashing the party."

Gemma caught a whiff of anger, and then it disappeared. She couldn't blame David for being angry. She was surprised he was being as nice as he was considering first Gemma and Sara, and now Mark, had intruded on his

18

evening. True, he had invited them to sit, but Sara hadn't really given him a choice.

David looked Mark squarely in the eye. "It's not my party." He seemed to take Mark's measure, and shrugged. "Pull up a chair. Take a load off."

Before Mark could sit Sara put her hand on his arm, and drew his attention back to her. "Come on, big boy. Let's see what moves you have." She began to dance her way through the tables to the dance floor. Mark placed his beer on the table, and followed her bouncy rear end.

Gemma reached for the beer in front of her. She offered David a shy smile. "Looks like you're stuck with me." Her voice nearly squeaked, she was so nervous, and that only made her more self-conscious.

David lips curved slowly into a smile. Gemma's heart did a curious little flip-flop. Damn, he was cute.

"I don't think being stuck with you will be such a hardship," he said.

His voice was husky, with the promise of things to come. Gemma suddenly found her beer bottle fascinating. This should be interesting. Her first beer. She took a small sip, and sputtered, nearly spitting it out. How could anyone drink this stuff? It was horrid!

She knew David struggled to keep from laughing out loud. "Is there a problem with your beer?" he asked.

Gemma felt the heat rise to her cheeks. "No." She ran her fingers through her bangs, and shook her head letting them fall back into place. "At least I don't think there is. It's just, I didn't expect it to be so bitter."

"Oh. That's all." David signalled to a nearby waitress. "There's a quick remedy for that." When the waitress came he asked her for a glass, and a saltshaker. He didn't say a word until the waitress returned. Gemma was grateful for the chance to pull herself back together.

David winked at the waitress. "Thanks. You may have just saved the life of a future beer drinker." He reached for Gemma's beer. "May I?"

She hesitated, and then nodded. Gemma was fascinated with the way his fingers held the glass as he slowly poured the beer. They were such long, slender fingers. She wondered what they would feel like on her body. David looked up. His grin was wicked, almost like he could read her mind. This time the heat began below her belly, and spread.

David's hand trembled as he sprinkled salt into her beer, and handed the glass back to Gemma. "Try this."

Gemma accepted the glass, and concentrated on the tiny bubbles rising through the amber liquid. Once again under control, she cautiously took a sip. She was pleasantly surprised. "I'd never have thought salt would make such a difference." She took a couple more swallows of beer, and began to relax.

"Do you live around here, David?"

"No. I'm just here on vacation. A friend told me about the Wolf Center and I thought I'd check it out."

"When are you going? I work there. Maybe I can show you around."

"Wish I'd known that before." He looked her up and down. His grin was wicked, and Gemma's cheeks burned. "I was there yesterday. I would remember seeing you."

Gemma turned her glass one-way, and then the other. Her eyes never left the tiny bubbles. "I was around," she mumbled, slightly disappointed.

They talked about the wolves at the center for a while, and Gemma accepted David's offer of another beer. She leaned back in her chair, and smiled. David was good company. The beer was cold, and she could get to like his flirting. She danced with David. She danced with Mark. She even danced with Sara.

Gemma was laughing when she and Sara came off the dance floor. "You're outrageous," she accused her friend.

"I'm serious," Sara told her. "I'm going to marry Mark." She turned to watch him make his way back from the washrooms. She licked her lips. "Yummy."

Gemma rolled her eyes. "And what does Mark say about that?"

"Oh, I haven't told him yet." They were still laughing when Mark reached the table and sat down.

Gemma wiped the tears from her cheeks, and took a big swallow of beer. "Wow." She set the glass on the table, and licked her lips. "I put way too much salt in this one." She scrunched up her nose. Something smelled—off. "Oh well," she said, and took another swallow. "Don't want to waste it." They all laughed again.

Gemma tried to focus on Sara and Mark while they danced. It wasn't easy. The way they kept weaving in and out amongst the other dancers was making her dizzy. She blinked, and rubbed the back of her neck. She shook her head and tried to clear the cobwebs. Her mouth was dry. She reached for her beer, and took another cool drink of the amber liquid. She was drinking an awful lot of beer. The more she drank the thirstier she got. The thirstier she got, the more she drank. Funny how that worked. Gemma was finding it harder and harder to focus.

David stood beside her chair looking at her, and Gemma squinted up at him. "Is there something on my nose?"

"Come on, Caitlin," he said. "It's time to go."

"Go?" Gemma forced her eyes open wide, and looked around the room. "Go where?" And who was Caitlin? What was wrong with her? She couldn't even string two words together to make a sentence.

"Home."

Gemma struggled a little when David took her arm. "Where's home?" She couldn't think. She looked around the room but everything was blurry. The coloured lights made her dizzier, if that was possible. Oh yeah, now she remembered. "Where's Sara?"

"Sara left with Mark." David steered her towards the back door. "She asked me to drive you home."

That couldn't be right. Sara was right there. Dancing with Mark. Or was she? Gemma couldn't see her anywhere. Maybe she did go home with Mark.

The cool night breeze slapped her face. Gemma stumbled on the steps. David put his arm around her, and pulled her closer to him. He lowered his head, and murmured softly to her. Gemma snuggled close.

"This way." He led her towards the back of the parking lot. "My van is over here." He had parked in a spot in the far corner of the parking lot. The light in that corner was broken, leaving the cars there in shadow.

"I don't feel so good." It came out 'I don' feels good' and Gemma began to giggle. What was wrong with her? She felt so strange. She tried to lift her head from where it was resting under his shoulder, but it was such a chore. Besides, he smelled so good, like a spicy muffin. Her stomach growled. She snuggled closer, and yawned.

"Here we are, sleepy head." David slid the side door open easily, and half lifted Gemma into the back of the van.

Gemma struggled to focus on her surroundings. It was so dark inside the van. Normally she had excellent night vision but tonight she couldn't see her hand in front of her face. Maybe it was because the windows were painted over. Strange. Why would anyone want to paint the windows? She really didn't like how the beer was making her feel. It was doing crazy things to her thinking. She spied a mattress against the opposite wall. Perfect. She was so tired. Gemma stumbled to the mattress, and was sleeping before David turned the key in the ignition.

She was having the most erotic dream. He was a musician, and she was his violin—wound so taut she could break any second.

"Wake up, sleepyhead."

His voice was gentle, making her feel warm and safe. She struggled to open her eyes. Blinked them shut then open again. Everything had a decidedly pinkish tinge. This was different than her usual dreams. She liked it.

There was movement on her right. She quickly turned her head only to be mesmerized by the bluest eyes. Her tongue darted out, and licked her suddenly dry lips. For the first time she was seeing her dream lover's face. He was gorgeous. His lips parted in a wickedly knowing smile, and her heart flip-flopped. His chest was bare and smooth. She watched fascinated as his long slender fingers undid the button on his jeans. What would it feel like to have those fingers touching her? Caressing her bare skin?

"… most … delicious … dream." She sighed.

"That's right, baby. You're dreaming."

His eyes were hypnotic. They held hers while he gently straddled her. His warm fingers brushed feather light against her bare flesh. Funny. She didn't usually sleep in the nude.

"What are you doing?" It came out 'whaya doin', and Gemma giggled.

"Hush." His voice was a gentle whisper. "I'm going to make all your dreams come true."

His fingers barely skimmed the surface of her skin. She was so hot. She was sure she would burst into flames. The muscles in her abdomen clenched. Her breath came in short rapid pants. Slowly, ever so slowly, he moved his hands in a circular motion above her nipples, barely touching. She never wanted to wake up.

"Please." She pleaded in a husky whisper. Not sure if she was begging him to stop, or continue. A voice inside her head screamed. *"Stop. This is wrong."* The voice sounded a lot like her mother's. Her body quivered with excitement. *"Shut up,"* she told the voice. *"Stay out of my dreams."*

His heated fingers barely stroked her feverish body. Her nipples grew. They stretched, lengthened, reached for the palms of his hands. They begged for his touch. Gemma gasped when his warm fingers obligingly cupped her breasts, and began to gently knead them. His thumbs, rough and warm, teased her taunt nipples, making them grow even more. She wanted to reach out and caress him, but she was afraid. Afraid that if she touched him she would wake up, and he would disappear with the dawn's early rays.

"You like that, don't you?" he crooned. "That's okay, baby." Just the sound of his voice had her quivering with desire. "You don't have to say a word. I know what you need."

Gemma stared at his mouth in fascination. The way his tongue barely touched his lips made her wonder what it would be like to feel those lips pressed against hers. She licked her own, dry lips, and tried to calm the erratic beating of her heart.

Gemma gasped breathlessly as his mouth moved ever so slowly towards hers. His teeth tugged gently on her lower lip. Then his tongue followed the path her own had recently taken, before darting between her parted lips to explore the heated cavern inside. He lifted his mouth from hers all too quickly. Gemma nearly cried in disappointment, until she felt the whisper of warm breath fluttered wing-like across her naked skin, and his lips moved to take the place of his hands. He caught her swollen nipple between his teeth gently tugging and teasing before taking the whole thing into his mouth, and suckling. Her body quivered helplessly. His heat seared her tender flesh. The bed moved slightly as he shifted position. His fingers slowly, torturously mapped a trail over the clenched muscles of her abdomen. Liquid heat pooled deep in her center.

All rational thought flew out the window.

He continued to suckle at her breast, while his fingers moved lower to tease her small nub mercilessly. Never before had her dreams been so erotic—so wanton.

Her body writhed beneath his, allowing him the freedom to do as he pleased. Her body screamed for his fiery touch.

Her legs opened wider at his prodding, giving him full access to her heated core. She cried out as one long finger slid inside. Her body was on fire. Her dreams had never taken her so far before. She hovered on the edge of climax.

She wanted more of him—needed all of him.

Her dream lover positioned himself between Gemma's legs. Gently he probed her moist opening with the tip of his manhood. She spread her legs further at his urging, and he thrust into her, burying his throbbing shaft into her moist heat.

Gemma screamed as a sudden, fiery pain tore her apart.

His mouth covered hers, capturing her screams. He began to thrust faster, and harder—and deeper.

Gemma tried to wake up.

She bucked, and twisted in her attempts to throw him off. She thought she would die from the pain. Gemma tried to concentrate but the agony was unbearable. It wouldn't stop.

Gemma tried to pull him off. She raked his back with claw-like nails. He released her lips, and grabbed her arms, forcing them above her head. She snarled at him. Her swollen lips curled above her even teeth. She snapped at him. And missed.

He roared as he spilled his seed into her, a roaring river of molten lava, and slumped across her.

Gemma sunk her canines deep into his shoulder.

It was his turn to scream.

*****

If the jackhammers stopped she might get back to sleep. The scent of fresh earth washed over her. Gemma shivered. She reached for the sheet, and came back with a handful of dried leaves.

Leaves!

Her eyes shot open, and she sat up. Pain stabbed at her temples forcing her to lie back down.

Where was she?

Gemma couldn't remember leaving the bar. Actually, she didn't remember too much about the bar at all.

What was that strange metallic taste? Cautiously, Gemma opened first one eye, and when the jackhammers didn't return, the other. She was lying in a thicket, naked. *Great!* She must have shifted after leaving the bar last night. *Where were her clothes?*

Obviously they were somewhere between the bar and here...wherever here was. The other obvious question was whether they were neatly folded somewhere waiting for Gemma to return and put them on, or shredded beyond repair.

Elizabeth was teaching her to use the magic when she shifted to save her clothes, but she wasn't very good at it. More often than not she would send her clothes away, but not get them back when she became human again. Gemma sat up slowly, and looked around the thicket, not surprised that her clothes were nowhere to be found.

She tried to conjure up a shirt, but the pain in her head was so intense she couldn't concentrate. Bile rose in her throat, and she spewed the contents of her stomach all over the ground.

She had to get home before someone found her like this. It was several more minutes before she was able to stand on her own. Slowly, one agonizing step after another, she made her way out of the thicket to find herself outside the main gates to the wolf center. Her office was there, and in her office was a spare change of clothes.

Thanking her lucky stars, Gemma clamoured over the fence to drop unladylike on the other side. She would get dressed, and go home to bed.

Chapter Four

The heat was oppressive. The sun beat down, hurting his eyes behind the dark glasses. The heat wasn't the only thing making sweat trickle down his back and soak his shirt. Guilt was a big part of it.

For a moment he actually considered rejecting Manuel's offer, but something about this country spoke to him. It screamed home like nowhere else had. He shifted uncomfortably, and tried to focus on what Father Augusto Hernandez was saying as he laid to rest the tortured souls of the Martinez family.

Father Hernandez had given the last rights before the bodies were cremated, and had agreed to perform the ceremony for Alicia's benefit. Jade believed that the child needed to see her parents put to rest, and because she was paying for everything, nobody objected.

"Is there something on your mind, Matt?" Jade's voice was barely a whisper, yet Matthew had no trouble hearing.

He glanced at her. Her unique amber eyes were swirling with emotion, and her luscious lips were curled into a mysterious, knowing smile. Matthew tore his dark gaze from her brighter one to stare across the open graves to the beckoning jungle beyond. The only person who truly loved the two people being put to rest today, sat silently in a wheelchair staring at nothing at all. The doctor's hadn't wanted them to take her from the hospital, but Jade had insisted that the child needed to be here.

"Do you really think it was a good idea to bring the girl?"

Jade's sigh whispered across the space between them. "We had to bring her. She needs to see her parents are at peace."

Matthew didn't think the child could *see* anything at all, but he believed in Jade. If she said the child knew what was happening around her, then Matthew believed it was true. Sweat trickled between his shoulder blades, and Matthew once again shifted position.

Father Hernandez spoke his final words. Manuel Rodriguez tossed a shovel of dirt onto each of the coffins. Jade took the limp roses from Alicia's idle hands, and toss one onto each of the two coffins. She took the handles of the chair, and pushed Alicia back to the rented van.

While Jade was securing Alicia in the van Matthew thanked Father Hernandez, and then hurried to drive them back to the hospital. Once Alicia was safely tucked into bed Jade motioned for the others to step out into the hallway. As soon as the door clicked shut she turned her attention on him. "So, Matthew. Now do you want to tell me what's on your mind?"

Matthew reached into his pocket, and pulled out a chocolate bar. Extending his hand palm up he offered it to Jade. "Brought you a treat."

Jade snatched the bar, tore off the paper, and stuffed it into her mouth. Then she slowly licked the sticky chocolate from each and every finger, licked off the paper making sure she got every drop, before crumpling the paper into a tight ball, and then handed it back to Matthew. She patted his front pockets. "Come on," she said as she continued to pat him down in her best imitation of a police officer. "Where do you have it stashed?"

Matthew's expression was one of quilt. "What?"

"You know better than to tease me like this."

Matthew squirmed. "I don't know what you're talking about."

Jade sat back on her heels, her hands in front of her, and her tongue hanging out. "I'm begging. Don't keep me begging."

Matthew laughed at her antics, and reached down to pull her back into a stand. "Okay." He threw his hands into the air in surrender. "I confess. I bought two, but I ate one on the way to the church."

Jade glared at him, hands on her hips. "Let me get this straight. You bought me two chocolate bars as a peace offering, because you obviously have something to say to me that you think I won't like. Then you *ate* one? You owe me Matt."

She was right. He did owe her; much more than a chocolate bar. Matthew owed Jade his life. Literally. If Jade hadn't rescued him from the lab at the Center for Psychic Research, he had no doubt that he would be dead right now.

Matthew was one of those rare *weres* to be born wolf. For the first twelve years of his life he lived in the forest with his father. Wild and free. He had known no other life than that of a wolf. Even after he received his magic, and began to shift he preferred to run around the forest on all fours. His mother had died in childbirth, and his father had no desire to live among humans. If his father was even aware of the rumours of a wild child in the forest, he ignored them.

One sunny day during his twelfth summer Matthew was chasing a rabbit when he had his first encounter with humans. He had pounced on a rabbit, missed, and landed in a trap. Snarling and snapping, he struggled to free himself. It hadn't even occurred to him to shift and remove the trap. Unable to pull his paw free, he began to gnaw on it, determined to rid himself of the large metal trap. He was so intent on freeing himself that he didn't hear the approach of the hunters.

A snapping twig was his first warning. Matthew spun around to face this new threat. Blood, fur, and bits of bone spew from his mouth, and his lips curled in a warning snarl. He eyed the humans warily as one of them raised a large metal stick to his shoulder. There was a bang, a flash of light, and a burning sensation in his shoulder. Then his whole world went black, and Matthew crumpled to the ground.

He woke up in a small white room. He was groggy, and his head felt like it was going to split into a million pieces. There was a small window too high to reach, and a bowl of strange smelling water. He drank only when the thirst was too strong to ignore. It was then, when his limps refused to obey, and he couldn't lift his head, that they would come in with their needles, and scissors to take their samples.

In his weakened state it took much longer than usual for his wounds to heal, but eventually his body ejected the bullet, and his shoulder healed. Even his half chewed off limb completely healed itself. When the change came over him, his captors were ecstatic. They came more often after that to poke and prod, and take his blood. At first they tried to communicate with him while he was in human form. Matthew hated them with their long needles, and sharp knives. He refused to stand on two feet in their presence, and would only answer in growls and snarls.

Eventually they gave up trying to communicate with him. Believing him incapable of understanding, they began to speak freely around him. He listened to everything they said, using the information to help plan his escape from this hell.

Then he'd seen her. Jade. She was with a group of researchers brought in to observe him, but she was different from the rest. She pretended interest in everything the doctors were saying, but the whole time she spoke to him with her mind. Only once did she look directly at him.

That night she came back, and freed him from his prison. She took him home with her, and taught him how to live as a human, while allowing him the freedom to live like the wolf he was. If it wasn't for Jade, Matthew would be dead because there was no way he would ever become the weapon those men had wanted him to be.

Matthew owed Jade his life, and he wouldn't desert her now.

"I do owe you," he said in his soft-spoken voice, which was in such contrast to his hard muscled body. "More than you'll ever know."

Jade smiled then. Really smiled. Her smile could fill a room with light, and bring a grown man to his knees. Her smile could make anyone, or anything, want to do her bidding. "What is it, Matthew?"

Matthew shuffled his feet, and fought the urge to confess what he so desperately wanted. "Nothing. I was just thinking about when we met, and how much I owe you."

"You don't owe me anything, Matthew." Jade paused for a second, searching Matthew's face intently. She didn't attempt to search his mind, or he would have known. "I thought you had something you wanted to tell me."

Matthew's heart twitched. Jade was his only family. After she had rescued him from his prison, they had returned to his den in the forest to find the decaying remains of his father. Unable to subdue the fully-grown werewolf as easily as they had his pup, they had decapitated him, cut out his heart, and left his remains, unaware than none of the forest creatures would dine on the flesh of a werewolf. Matthew was torn between his desire to stay, and his desire to stay with Jade.

"I have a confession." Jade gave a quick glance in his direction, and then dropped her eyes. "I need someone to stay here in Mexico, and help protect these people. I can't be everywhere at once, and you know how much I hate flying."

Matthew laughed. The only flying Jade hated was in an airplane, and they both knew it. Hope flared as he realized where she was heading. "And you want me?"

"I know it's an imposition. I know how much you hate being human."

"I don't exactly hate it." Even as Matthew spoke the words out loud, he realized they were true. Another thing he owed to Jade. She had taught him to embrace both sides of his nature. He may prefer his animal side but he no longer despised his human counterpart.

"I'm glad to hear that." Jade glanced in at the girl lying so still in the bed, and then turned her attention back to Matthew. "How would you like to head up the Mexican division of O'Connell Search and Rescue?" She held up her hand when Matthew started to speak. "Before you say anything, hear me out. All the necessary visas have been obtained. I have purchased the farm we are renting. There are hundreds of acres of jungle for you to run in. You are far enough away from town for privacy, and close enough that you can keep your eye on things. You will be working closely with Manuel. He has an open mind, and I would trust him with my life. How much you trust him with is up to you. But I would count him as a friend. So what do you say?"

It was perfect. Maybe a little too perfect. Matthew looked at Jade suspiciously, but as far as he could tell she wasn't hiding anything. Suddenly Matthew didn't want to stay. He scrambled around in his head before he hit on the perfect reason not to stay. "I can't stay. Who'd do all the driving?" Jade had never learned to drive. She had hired someone else to teach him.

Jade sucked in her bottom lip, betraying her own nervousness. "That brings me to my confession. I have an interview with that young man from Willow Bend. Daniel Dixon. He has sent me several letters, and I just felt it was time to meet him."

"Really?" Matthew glared at Jade, but she just watched him with those calm, amber eyes. "When did this happen?"

"This morning. I rang him from the farm while you were out running, and apparently eating my chocolate bar." She narrowed her eyes at him sternly, and then shrugged. "He has agreed to meet with me in two weeks. I have a good feeling about this, Matthew. I'm sure he will work out."

"In that case I accept your offer."

They both knew he would. There had never really been a question of his leaving.

Chapter Five

What had that bitch done to him?

David carefully removed the bloodied bandage from his shoulder. He used the mirror to see to clean the wound. Stupid bitch. She's lucky he hadn't killed her. He could have crushed her windpipe with just a bit more pressure. He probably would have if it weren't for that damned medallion she was wearing. He looked at the image of the wolf seared into his thumb, and cursed again. He hoped she was wondering about the bruise on her neck.

He applied antibiotic cream on the bite, as well as on his thumb. He was lucky. It wasn't nearly as bad as he'd first thought. There had been so much blood he'd thought she had ripped his shoulder right off. As it was, there wasn't much of a mark. Just a red blotch.

Damn the girl! This was all her fault. The moment she'd entered the room she had him acting out of character. The way her hand had gone to her bangs. The sexy sway of her hips as she'd crossed the room. It had all been calculated to make him want her.

It worked! He'd wanted her so badly he had broken all his own rules.

David covered the wound with a clean bandage, and popped two more painkillers into his mouth. It might not look bad but it hurt like hell. He drank a glass of orange juice, washed the glass, and set it on the drain board. God, his head was splitting. He hoped the bite wasn't infected. He had read somewhere that a human's bite could be much worse than a dog's. It hadn't looked infected, but he would check it again tonight.

He grabbed his lab coat off the hook, and made sure the door locked behind him. If he didn't hurry he was going to be late for work.

Chapter Six

Jade sat beside the hospital bed, and held the child's hand. She talked to her about the weather, the birds singing in the trees, her Da back home in the States. Alicia lay in the bed, motionless. She stared straight ahead without blinking. She might have been sleeping, except her eyes were open. The doctor and nurses went about their business, checking IV's and vital signs, adjusting this tube and that. Even they were at a loss. "She's in shock." The doctor shrugged, and gave Jade a half-hearted smile. "She'll wake when she's ready. There is nothing to do. Just keep her comfortable."

Jade sat with her, talked to her, worried about her. She looked into those black, empty eyes, and wondered where the child was. If only Althea were here. Althea would know what to do.

Talk to her, Jade. Let her know you are there, waiting for her to come back.

Jade listened to the familiar voice with her mind. She held the child's limp hand in hers, and reached out to the cosmos. She sought any trace of the voice that had screamed for help.

Mama. Where are you, mama? The mind voice was so sad, so lost, and Jade's heart melted.

It's time to come back. Jade called to the child. She reached out, and then she waited. After several, timeless moments, the child reached back.

*****

Alicia sat on the edge of the hospital bed. Her short legs swung back and forth. Her fingers were clenched in the top sheet. Her knuckles were white. *I won't talk to her.*

"It doesn't matter," Jade answered the small voice in her head. She picked up a blue denim dress with a knitted, pink bear sewn on the front.

"This is nice." She held the dress up to Alicia. Her head was tilted on a slight angle as she looked it up, and down. "Don't you think?"

Alicia's face darkened. *It's ugly.* She turned her head towards the window.

Jade was silent as Alicia's eyes blinked several times. The child could be so stubborn. Jade wanted to wrap her arms around her, and protect her from what was coming, but she couldn't. If she was going to heal, Alicia had to face what had happened to her parents. Face what had almost happened to her. All Jade could do now was surround her with the people who could help her heal, and teach her about her powers.

A grackle whistled from its perch outside the open window. Alicia took a deep breath, and turned watery eyes in Jade's direction. *You can't make me talk to her.*

"I know." Since she'd woken up Alicia hadn't spoken out loud, not even to Jade. "I also know that if you don't start talking people are going to think I'm crazy for talking to myself, and want to lock me up."

Jade folded the dress, and added it to the growing pile of discarded clothing beside the still empty suitcase. She held up a white, frilly dress with blue flowers. "So?" She shook the dress in front of Alicia. "What about this?"

Alicia's lips twitched. "Where did you find this stuff?"

Jade smiled. Her eyes danced with amusement. She wasn't sure Alicia realized it, but the child had actually spoken. Out loud. "I thought you'd like it," she said. "I thought you were one of those girly girls."

Alicia smiled for the first time since she woke up. "You're like mama." Tears pooled in her dark eyes, and she sniffled. She let go of the sheet, and jumped off the bed. Her small hands reached for a pair of plain denim jeans, like the ones Jade was wearing.

"I like these," she said. She held them up against her small frame. About four inches of material lay on the floor in front of her. "I'll grow into them." She bobbed her head up and down. "Yeah. I can grow this much."

"Why wait. If you like them I can cut the bottoms off for you," Jade told her. "That way you can wear them now."

Alicia burst into tears. She tossed the jeans into the suitcase, and turned to clutch the front of Jade's shirt. "Where is Mama?" The shirtfront muffled her words. "Why isn't she here?" She sniffed, tipped her head back, wiped the end of her nose, and stared at Jade with black, watery eyes. *What did I do? Why did she go away? It's my fault, isn't it? She's mad 'cause I couldn't save Papa?*

"You didn't do anything, Sweetheart." Jade felt her own eyes burn with unshed tears. The poor child. She was so little. At eight she could easily pass for five. She was like a little cherub, with her mass of black, curly hair framing her face, and bunching at her shoulders. She looked so forlorn, so alone. She didn't deserve this. No child deserved this.

Jade's heart was breaking. For the first time, in a very long time, Jade wished she were normal. She'd take this precious little girl in a heartbeat. Love her ,and care for her like she deserved.

But Jade wasn't normal. She had a job to do, and that didn't include caring for a child; any child. Jade's eyes burned. Whether for this child or the child she would

39

probably never have, she wasn't entirely sure. She squatted down, and pulled Alicia into her arms. She forced a smile in her voice. "You'll like Althea," she told her. "And the Murphys will adore you."

"I like you!"

"I know honey. I like you too."

Alicia pushed herself back so she was once again looking into Jade's face. "Let me come with you."

"We've been through this." Jade sighed. She couldn't expect the child to understand why she couldn't take her. She needed special help. Eventually she was going to remember what happened, and when she did she would need all the help she could get. Help from someone who knew what the girl had been through. From someone who knew the truth. "I can't take you with me. You need to go where there is someone to look after you. I can't do that when I am working. I travel a lot, and I never know when I will be home. Althea loves children. And she will know exactly what you need. She will stay with you as long as you need her."

Unshed tears made her voice rough. "Come on. Let's finish your packing. Althea will be here any moment."

"You're just like everyone else." Alicia flung her arm out, and knocked the suitcase to the floor. "Mama doesn't want me, and you don't want me. Nobody wants me."

Jade scooped the child into her arms, holding her struggling frame gently, but firmly until she went limp. Then she sat on the edge of the bed, the sobbing child on her lap, and rocked her back and forth. How did you tell a child whose entire world had just come crashing down, that you had to send her away?

"You're wrong, Sweetheart." Jade tried to keep her own voice calm, but it cracked. "Your mother loved you very much. She would have done anything for you. I would do anything for you."

The door swung open silently. A tall, slender woman entered the room. She could have been Jade's twin. They were almost identical, but for the hair. The newcomer's fell to her waist in a dark, golden flow. She watched her niece rock the small child, and she knew what was in the other woman's heart. "Looks like I'm just in time."

Jade stopped rocking at the sound of the familiar voice. *¡Váyase!*

Althea stepped back. The push to go away was strong. She drew herself up to her full height, and took two more steps into the room. She ignored the child for now. "Do you have a hello for your favourite Aunt?"

Alicia's hands clenched into small fists, and her brow furrowed. *I said, go away.*

"You're right," Althea said. She ignored the child, looking at Jade when she spoke. "She is strong." It was a full minute before she turned her attention to the child. "How long have you been able to do that?" she asked in the child's own language. She could have picked the answer out of the child's mind, but that wasn't the way to win her trust.

Alicia buried her face in Jade's shirt. She put her hands over her ears.

"I see she doesn't want to talk." Althea picked the suitcase off the floor, and set it on the bed. She picked up the jeans, making a big production of shaking them out, smoothing them down, folding them neatly, and putting them in the empty suitcase. She ignored most of the other clothes scattered on the floor, choosing a baggy sweatshirt, a pair of green shorts, and a plain white T-shirt. These she folded, and put in the suitcase. She closed the lid, and snapped the locks.

"Are the papers in order?" she asked Jade.

Jade took inventory, "passport, airplane tickets, and temporary custody papers."

"Are you sure you know what you're doing?"

Jade stared into Althea's eyes. *She has nobody else.* "You're the only one who can help her." Her strange, amber eyes pleaded for understanding.

"I know that!" Althea took a deep breath, and blew out slowly through pursed lips. "I would have come without your call."

It was the simple truth. Althea had a gift for healing both the minds, and the bodies of those touched by evil. She always knew where she was needed, and like Jade, Althea would never hesitate to use those gifts. What Jade didn't know, was that Althea was more worried about Jade's state of mind than that of the troubled child.

Althea held the eye contact. Using their special connection she asked, *Are you sure about the adoption?*

"You want to adopt me?" Alicia sat up, her small head turning from Jade to Althea, and back again.

Althea cocked an eyebrow in her direction. The child was a natural. She could see why Jade was so concerned about her. "Well, what do you know? She can talk." She didn't mention the fact that Alicia had been listening to their private conversation.

Jade on the other hand, did. "It's not nice to listen to other people's thoughts?" She narrowed her eyes, trying to look stern.

"Oops. Sorry." Alicia looked to the floor, but not before Jade saw the sparkle in her dark eyes. She swung her legs back and forth. Then her head popped up, and her face broke into a grin. "But you want to adopt me? Right?"

Jade cocked her head to one side, and studied the child. At this moment it was only an idea. One she wasn't sure would ever become a reality. Who was she kidding, anyway? There was no way she could care for a small child—at least, not yet. "I can't," she finally said. There was no sense getting the child's hopes up "Althea has been given temporary custody of you." It hadn't been hard to get custody. With no living relatives, there was nobody to pay her bills. There had been nobody willing to take the child in.

Sure, they had made a token fuss. After all, Jade was proposing to take one of their own out of the country. In the end, the judge was happy to sign the custody papers. Jade hadn't had to try very hard to persuade him. "She is taking you to the States, where you will be staying with her, and Da. Remember, I told you about my—Grandfather." Da and Althea would keep the child safe, and the Murphys would treat her like one of their own. They had been with the O'Connells for almost twenty-five years. Jade had hired Mrs. Murphy through an agency to take care of her father when she had to be away. Mr. Murphy had come along to help with the yard, and the dogs. Together, they kept things running while Jade was away. She trusted them with more than just her home. They were family.

Alicia started to protest. Jade set her on the floor and stood up. "Da raised me after my own parents were gone. You'll love him. He can hardly wait for you to get there. He's already talking about giving you your own dog."

She gathered the clothing scattered on the floor, and dumped them on the bed. "We'll leave these here. Maybe the Sisters can give them to somebody who will appreciate them."

Althea glanced pointedly at the clock on the wall. "We have to leave if we are going to catch the plane."

"I'm not going."

Alicia stood in front of the hospital bed, her dark skin pale, her eyes bigger than saucers, her legs spread out, and her hands on her hips. Jade grabbed her own pack from beside the door, and slipped her arms through the straps. She grabbed the suitcase from the bed in one hand, and held the other one out to Alicia who stared at it for several seconds. Her shoulders slumped, and she placed her small hand in Jade's. The three left the hospital room together.

While Althea showed proof of temporary custody, and signed Alicia out of the hospital, the nurses flocked around the child offering their sympathy. Alicia stared straight ahead, eyes focused on something that nobody else could see. She didn't acknowledge their presence by word or action.

When they finally gave up and left her alone, she put one foot in front of the other, looking neither left nor right, and headed for the door.

"Poor thing" ... "the same" ... "losing her parents" ... "horrible" ... Snatches of conversation floated towards them, and Jade quickened the pace.

They pushed the front door open and stepped outside. Jade gasped. It was so hot. The air was sucked from her lungs. She wiped her fingers across her eyelids. The heat rolled and shimmered above the pavement. There wasn't a hint of breeze. The heat didn't seem to affect Alicia. She just put one foot in front of the other, and kept on walking. All fight gone. Althea, on the other hand, looked ready to drop.

"Taxi?"

Althea shrugged.

"I like the bus." The voice was barely a whisper on the non-existent breeze, but both women heard it, and smiled.

There were three taxis waiting in front of the hospital. The driver's were slumped in their seats, hats tilted over their brows. The first in line sat up and signalled them. Jade waved him back down. There was a bus heading in the right direction. Jade stepped onto the road and raised two fingers. The bus pulled over and stopped. Jade lifted Alicia on to the first step and gave her a small push forward. Althea had one foot on the second step when the driver shoved the bus into gear, and then pulled out in front of another bus. There wasn't time to dally if he was going to make his money.

"*Tres para el aeropuerto, por favor,*" Jade said. She had to grab the railing to keep from falling as the driver took a bend way too fast. Althea slipped past her and followed Alicia.

"*Cuarenta y cinco pesos,*" the driver said. He switched gears, and the bus went faster.

Jade held the pole in a death grip with one hand while she counted out coins with the other. She dropped fifty pesos in the container and looked for Alicia. Of course she would have to be on the very back seat. Her grin, stretching from ear to ear as the bus bounced and rattled, made it all worthwhile.

"Figures she'd pick the back," mumbled Jade.

"*Perdón?*"

Jade gave the driver one of her dazzling smiles. "*Nada,*" she told him and started for the back of the bus. The bus lurched. Jade grabbed the nearest seat to keep from being thrown down. Compared to this, hunting was a walk in the park. She finally reached the back and sat down with an exaggerated sigh.

"The back's the best," Alicia said, undaunted by the looks of the grownups on each side of her.

"Of course it is," Althea said. She winked at Jade. "You get to feel every bump from back here."

At that precise moment the bus hit a large bump and Jade grabbed the back of the nearest seat to keep from being flung to the floor. As soon as she regained her seat the bus came to an abrupt halt, throwing her forward again. The next victim was no sooner on the first step then the bus lurched forward again. Alicia laughed with glee. The locals all seemed to take it in stride, smiling and greeting each other, as the bus rolled from side to side. All the trees were clipped at the edge of the road on one side, while on the other, the side Jade was sitting on, the road dropped down a sheer cliff to the roiling ocean.

Jade held her breath on one corner when she saw a car coming towards them cut across the center of the road. The bus driver didn't slow down. He just pulled the bus further towards the edge of the cliff and stepped harder on the gas. Jade would have sworn the back wheels were airborne.

Jade wasn't afraid of much. Until now, she would have thought flying in a plane was it. It was stupid, really. She had nothing to worry about, personally. But if the bus crashed, Alicia, and the other passengers, wouldn't be so lucky. She watched Alicia. She stared out the window watching the trees fly by, like pickets on a fence, and she laughed. Alicia loved this. It was evident on her animated face. Jade preferred other methods of travel.

This just wasn't safe.

The rear exit door was swinging open and closed, the latch long since broken off. There wasn't a window on the right-hand side of the bus without a crack. Some were completely missing. The front window had a crack that ran from the top right hand corner to the bottom left. Jade was sure that it impaired the driver's vision. A nativity set was mounted just above the dash, and below that was a sign *'Vaya con Dios!'* 'Go with God.' One day she hoped to—Just not today.

Jade leaned back in her seat, closed her eyes, and forced herself to relax. The bus came to one of its sudden stops and Althea poked Jade in the shoulder. "Come on, sleepy head," she teased.

Apparently the airport was the end of the line for the buses; At least temporarily. The driver actually put the bus in park, opened the doors, and left the bus. The trio gathered their stuff and exited the bus with most of the others. A couple of passengers leaned back in their seats, closed their eyes, and prepared to wait for the driver's return.

The small airport was crowded. There were so many people the air conditioning had no effect at all. The beginnings of a headache scratched at Jade's temples. Emotions were running high. Tension filled the small airport. People were anxious to get home after their holidays. They were frustrated with the long line ups that moved at a snail's pace. Jade pressed the heel of her hand against her temple and tried to make her mind blank. She hated crowds. Give her wide-open, sparsely populated spaces, and she was in heaven. This was hell for her.

Jade forced herself to focus on a heavyset man in the line in front of them. He took his hat off to fan his face. He wiped the back of his hand across his forehead and plunked his hat back on top of his head. He pushed the luggage piled in front of him ahead a few inches and looked around. A couple of minutes later he repeated the process. Just as he reached the counter, his wife and daughter joined him, laden with parcels, and he sighed.

It was their turn. Jade waited while Althea handed over the tickets, the passports and the temporary custody papers, for herself and Alicia. The man at the counter lifted an eyebrow at the lack of luggage. A single suitcase for two people wasn't much. He didn't say a word.

Alicia looked at Jade, her pack still hanging from her shoulders. She didn't say a word. Jade hoped she was finally accepting the fact that she was going with Althea.

An old man with a gray beard about six inches long and wearing a ragged baseball cap kept looking at them and scribbling on a piece of paper. He cautiously approached them where they stood in line to buy a drink. "Excuse," he said. His breath smelled of cigarette smoke and his voice was raspy.

He pushed a four by six piece of paper towards them. "You like?" he asked.

Jade took the paper from the man who was shoving it at her.

It was beautiful.

The charcoal black, pencil strokes had captured their very essence. She could see the dark, golden tresses which fell past Althea's waist. Extra strokes had produced the masses of black curls tumbling from Alicia's head and bunching around her shoulders. Lighter strokes were used to represent Jade's short-cropped, pale hair, with its streaks of silver and gold.

The eyes grabbed you. In just those few minutes, the man had seen their secrets and they showed in the eyes.

Althea's eyes were ancient and kind, keeping the worlds secrets. Alicia's, huge, dark and filled with fear and loss. Jade's eyes were full of conflict. Shadows and lines depicted the battle she waged within herself. Jade could understand how the natives could believe that a picture could steal your soul.

"You like?" the man persisted.

"Oh." Jade dragged her eyes from the picture and looked at the artist. His eyes were black, like Alicia's. He tipped his head down to watch his toe as he kicked his old worn work boot at an imaginary spot on the floor. His weathered face was covered in lines and cracks. It was a face used to laughing. If Jade had to guess, she would put him at sixty, at least, maybe more. Right now his eyes kept flickering from the floor to his left, then to his right, then back to the floor.

A young man, probably in his early twenties, and wearing a brown airport security uniform, headed in their direction.

"You like?" the man persisted.

"Yes. I do," Jade told him. "Very much. It is beautiful."

"You buy," he smiled at her. He was missing a couple of teeth and those left were yellowed. "One dollar." The man held out his hand, keeping one eye on the approaching guard.

Jade glanced once more at the picture. She glanced at the approaching guard. It didn't take a genius to realize she was going to be this man's last sale for the day. She handed the picture to Alicia and reached into her pocket. She pulled out a twenty-dollar bill.

The man, once again glanced toward the guard, then frantically waved the money away. "No. No," he insisted. "One dollar." He turned his hands up, showing his sketchpad and pencil. "No pesos."

Jade placed the bill in his empty hand, and rolled his callused fingers closed over it. Obviously he didn't rely on his art for a living. He started once again to protest. Jade smiled at him. The man's face lit up like a child in a candy shop who had just been told he can have whatever he wants.

"*Gracias. Gracias.*' The man bobbed his head several times; His smile growing wider with each nod.

"You do beautiful work," she told him. She glanced at the guard who had nearly reached them. "Go now." She gave the man a gentle push towards the nearest exit. "Thank you for the beautiful gift," she called out behind him, loud enough for the guard to hear.

Jade turned towards the guard as he was about to follow the old man, cruelty written all over his face. 'Excuse me," she said. She placed a hand on his arm as he made to pass them. "Could you please tell me where the ladies' room is?"

One smile from Jade and all thoughts flew out of the guard's head. He didn't notice the old man slip out the exit and out of his reach.

The loud speaker crackled and a tinny voice announced they were beginning to board their flight. The three walked towards the boarding gate, leaving the guard standing where he was, watching them go, with a stupid grin on his face.

"Well, kiddo," Jade bent down and pulled Alicia into her arms. "Looks like this is the end of the line for us. You be good for Althea and I'll be home as soon as I can." Alicia's eyes glistened with tears. Jade's eyes burned.

"No!" Alicia clung to Jade. Tears spilled over, dampening Jade's shirt. Her small body trembled with anguish.

Althea put her hands on the child's shoulders and gently pulled her back. "It's okay, little one," she said. "I will take good care of you." She turned her eyes towards her niece then. "We will see Jade again. I promise."

Alicia clung to Jade for a moment more, then allowed Althea to pull her away. She wiped at her tears with rapid, jerky movements, sniffed and stared at Jade. Her large, dark eyes screamed betrayal. Jade's breath caught in her throat and her heart thudded.

"It'll be okay," Althea said. Jade wasn't sure if the words were meant for her or Alicia, but she allowed them to comfort her.

Althea took Alicia's small hand in hers, took the boarding passes from her pocket, and headed to the checkpoint. Alicia slipped her hand from Althea's and ran back to Jade. She shoved the picture at her. "You keep it," she cried. "I don't want it."

She ran back to Althea, took her hand, and tugged Althea towards the gate.

She didn't look back.

Chapter Seven

If she didn't do something to relieve the pressure soon she was going to scream. Screaming might do it. Wouldn't that be cute! She giggled at the thought; A grown woman standing in the middle of a busy street screaming for no apparent reason. Then again, she sobered at the thought, maybe nobody would notice a woman screaming in the street. That might be normal in a city like this.

It was the relentless, silent screams that had her wound so tight.

She had to get out of the city. Away from the cries of a thousand tortured souls, begging for release from their own private hells. Then she could focus on where she was supposed to be.

She was so tired. Too tired to shift, and there weren't any buses this late at night; At least not one leaving the city. It was at times like this that Jade thought about learning to drive.

There was a knock at the door. "Room service," a man's voice announced.

Jade opened the door, and stood to one side to let the young man push the cart into the room. God, he was good looking. A blond-haired, blue-eyed Adonis, like everyone else working at this hotel. She had yet to see one person with any inferior qualities whatsoever. It might make a less secure person a little uncomfortable, surrounded by all these gorgeous specimens of humanity. Jade liked beauty. She surrounded herself with it whenever possible. Even when she had to stay in the city, she could find beauty somewhere. Like at this, her favourite hotel.

"If you require anything else ..." The boy had been busy setting the table by the large picture window, while Jade had been busy watching the way his body moved.

He had managed to produce a linen tablecloth, a china plate, a crystal glass, china teacup, a silver teapot, and silver serving dishes, all from his tiny cart. There was even a vase with a single pink rose, a tall, slender candle set on an old fashion candle holder, which he was now in the process of lighting, and a real linen napkin.

There was enough food for at least two people. For Jade, that was a start. She could always grab a burger later. Part of the price she paid for her gifts. She needed a lot of fuel to keep this body of hers going. Fortunately, she wasn't one of the poor souls who needed to drink blood to survive. She loved her food way too much.

Steam escaped through the small hole at the top of the plate warmer, carrying with it the tantalizing aroma of rare meat. Her lips turned up. She ran her tongue over her suddenly moist lips. Her stomach rumbled.

"Is that an offer?" she asked. Her voice was low, husky. She almost laughed when the boy turned red, and nearly tripped over his own feet when he hurried to the door. He had no way of knowing she was actually thinking of what lay beneath that silver lid.

He stopped at the door. The hotel may have hired him for his looks, but they insisted on proper training for all their staff, and his job wasn't finished. He pulled a black folder from his pocket, and opened it.

"Err ... Umm ... You need ..." He swallowed. "Sign here." He looked at her then, his young blue eyes confused and pleading. "Please," he said.

Maybe if he were a few years older, quite a few years older, she would have teased him a bit more to see where it might lead. But, alas, he was just a child. Jade took the folder, signed her name, and handed it back. She didn't release it completely until he looked up at her again. "I'll take that as a no," she said.

She waited until the door was closed before she allowed herself to laugh. That was fun. It was too bad that he was so very young though. It could have been, at least, interesting, if her tastes didn't lean more towards men than pretty boys.

Jade sat down and devoured the steak. Usually, she would have savoured every single morsel, enjoying the way the warmed blood trickled down her throat. Tonight, she barely took the time to notice the taste. She had never been able to eat while on a plane. Today was no exception. Once the steak, running with blood the way she preferred it, was gone she turned her attention to the oven baked potatoes and sautéed mushrooms. When she finished it was a struggle not to lick her plate.

The night beckoned her.

Spread out below her, in all its glitter, the city called. From her vantage point the city was beautiful. Jade knew, close up, it would be like any other city in any other county, with garbage on the streets, broken down buildings, and torn up roads. Every city had its good and its bad parts. And every city had its part where evil preyed. From where she stood tonight, all that glittered was gold. She wanted to relax, and let herself believe that it was true--just for tonight.

Jade wanted to howl at the moon. She wanted to soar through the skies.

She showered, changed into form fitting suede pants, and a pale silk blouse. The cool material caressed her skin.

Her nipples peaked. She checked her appearance in the full-length mirror on the bathroom door.

Oh yeah. The clothes worked. The pants cupped the cheeks of her ass. Her nipples strained against the thin material of her blouse, begging to be released, begging to be kissed. Her short-cropped hair, so pale it was almost white with streaks of silver and gold, curled forward to caress her small, elfin face. There would be no mistaking her purpose tonight.

Jade stacked the used dishes on the cart, and rolled it out into the hall. She locked the door, and then pushed the button for the elevator. Someone, somewhere in this city of over half a million people, was going to get laid tonight.

Chapter Eight

Luke pushed his empty plate away, wiped his mouth, or rather tried to wipe his mouth, on the too thin paper napkin. It caught in his beard and tore. He scowled at the waitress. His dark, thunderous looks must have been enough because she didn't bother to ask if everything was okay. She just grabbed his plate, and hurried away as quickly as possible mumbling something about bringing his bill.

It served him right. God only knew why he picked such a dive anyway; probably because it matched his mood. The windows were dirty and cracked. The wallpaper was covered in so much grease and grime it was anyone's guess what it had originally looked like, and it was torn and peeling in places. There was dirt on the floor and counter. The waitress wore a uniform that looked like it hadn't seen the inside of a washing machine in months, if ever.

The cook was worse. She had a cigarette hanging out the corner of her mouth, and when the ashes fell off she didn't even bother pretending to try to remove them from the pot of whatever she had boiling on the stove. Her hair, greasy and limp, was in no way contained by the hair net she had half-heartedly set on the top of her head.

His first instinct had been to turn around and get as far away from this place as possible. Only he knew what his instincts had been worth lately.

Nothing. *Nada.* Zilch.

So he had sat at the cleanest table he could find. He had almost smiled - it was more like a grimace - when the young waitress had wiped a dry cloth over the tabletop, knocking several crumbs to join those on the floor. Her sunny smile was out of place. She made a few attempts at conversation, finally giving up when all she got were a few grunts for her trouble.

Luke had ordered steak, rare, and was actually surprised by how good it tasted. That would explain why there were so many people willing to risk their health by eating in a place like this.

The waitress returned with his bill. She laid it on the table in front of him, shuffled her feet a couple of times, and said, "I hope everything was to your satisfaction, sir."

Luke had to admire her dedication to her job. He wasn't sure he would have bothered if the roles were reversed. He looked at her then. This time he really looked, and he saw that the uniform had been washed so much that it was a pale shadow of its original color, and although it was stained there were no new stains. Her hair was clean and tied with a ribbon in a tight pony that hung down her back, and even his rudeness couldn't completely dampen the sparkle in her blue eyes. She glowed from the inside out.

Luke smiled, actually allowed his lips to curve into a real, heart-felt smile, showing his almost obscenely perfect teeth. "The steak was delicious," he said. He glanced at the bill, pulled out two twenties from his pocket, and handed both to the girl. "Keep the change."

She looked at the bills and her eyes widened. "You've made a mistake, sir," she said. "A twenty more than covers the bill."

Luke grinned, that devastating grin of his that usually had women falling all over themselves to please him, and replied. "Just call it an apology for my earlier rude behaviour."

"But ..."

"No buts. I haven't had such a delicious steak since I left home." It was the truth. He pushed back his chair, rose to his full height, winked, and headed for the door. Behind him he heard the girl sigh. He smiled. Things were beginning to look up.

An hour later, he was sitting at the hotel bar, brooding into his half empty glass.

"Got fifty bucks, Mister?"

Luke turned towards the voice and nearly fell off his chair. *My God! She's a baby.* "How old are you?" he blurted.

The girl shaped her garishly painted lips into a pout, and blew him a kiss. Her dress was short enough to be indecent, on anyone. Her hair was pulled into two pigtails. She looked like a schoolgirl. She probably was.

"How old do you want me to be?" she countered.

"Old enough to know you should be safely tucked in bed this time of night," he growled at her. He'd been doing that a lot lately. Maybe Erzsébet was right, and he should get himself laid.

"Are you offering to tuck me in?"

"I don't tuck in babies." Luke turned back to his drink.

"Hell, Mister. I'm twenty-five."

Luke turned back to the girl. "Yeah," he snarled at her. "And I'm old enough to be your grandfather." *Several times over.*

He waited while the girl looked him up and down. Apparently she didn't think he was worth the trouble.

"Your loss," she shot at him. She started towards the other end of the bar.

Luke put his hand on her arm. She was obviously used to dealing with men. She just looked from his hand to his face, and back again, without saying a word.

"What do you charge for the whole night?" Luke couldn't believe what he was about to do.

"Three hundred," she said. "And I don't do no kinky stuff."

That makes two of us. Luke pulled out his wallet, and counted out three hundred dollars. Her eyes widened. For a minute he thought she was going to try to renegotiate. She didn't.

"There's only one catch." Luke held the money just out of her reach.

"I told you, Mister. No kinky stuff." She looked at the money. Probably more money than she had seen in a long time. Then she looked at Luke. Her eyes narrowed, and she chewed on her bottom lip. "Okay. What do I have to do?" She reached for the money.

"Go to bed."

The girl laughed. "What'd you think you were paying for Mister?" She smiled at Luke, licked her lips, and said. "It will be my pleasure."

"Alone."

"What!" The girl's eyes widened. She looked at Luke as if he were insane.

"Alone." Luke looked down at her fingers, wrapped around the money. "If you take this money, you will go home, alone. I don't want to see you again tonight."

The girl shrugged. "Whatever." She rolled her eyes. She sighed. "Figures. Someone as good looking as you had to be gay."

Luke was shocked. Gay! Him! He had a sudden urge to throw her down, and show her just how much of a man he was. He pushed his free hand through his hair. *What was he thinking? She was still a child.* He shoved the money at her, turned her around, and pushed her towards the door. "Home. Now," he ordered.

Luke turned back to the bar and downed his whiskey it one swallow. He was just about to order another when the sudden silence in the bar made him turn around.

Now she was more his style.

She was tall. Her pale hair framed her elfin features like a cloud. Her taut nipples strained at the tight fabric of her blouse. His mouth watered at the thought of those nipples in his mouth. The way her pants hugged and caressed every curve of her long legs as she moved towards him made him wish she were leaving so he could watch the way they were sure to caress her ass.

She walked with confidence. Sex poured off her in waves. It was in every step she took. Most women of her stature would try to downplay their height. Not her. She moved with poise and confidence. Even with her two-inch heels he was taller than her.

Luke caught the glitter of jewellery on her left ankle when she took a step. He looked at the symbols on the anklet, and a distant memory flickered and then was gone. He shrugged it off and slowly moved his eyes back up that luscious frame to her face.

Her eyes were a strange shade of amber. They seemed to swirl with mystery and secrets. He was instantly hard. If the child could see him now she would definitely know where his interests lie.

She stood in front of him. A dream wrapped in a woman's body. She chewed on her lower lip. On her it was sexy. Every male eye was on her, but she didn't seem to notice. She looked only at him.

He stood perfectly still as her strange eyes traveled his form from head to foot. The slow, determined movement was like a caress against his skin. Her eyes paused at his crotch.

She cocked her head. "Looks like I got here just in time." Her voice caressed him like a lover's hand. He grew harder, and almost winced. Almost.

"Depends?" He stood there, legs splayed; trying to give himself some much needed room. He pointedly looked at her straining nipples, and licked his lips. It was almost impossible to keep from leaning forward and running his tongue over the shiny fabric of her blouse.

"What did you have in mind?" He knew what she had in mind. It was written all over her. The woman was in heat. It rolled off her in waves. Her musky scent called to him. A call he intended to answer very soon. With the moon, and the scent of the woman pulling him he had no choice.

They circled each other in some bizarre mating ritual. It was a game. Nothing more. They both knew where it was going to end up.

Get out! Run! Before it's too late. A voice screamed in his head. *Shut up,* he answered. Maybe he should listen to the voice. Then, again, it hadn't been right in days.

He knew he looked good. He could see it in her amber eyes. The way they glowed when she looked at him. The way she licked her lips ever so slightly—like she couldn't wait to taste him.

"I'm pretty sure you can guess." She played her role well.

Luke grunted. "What's it going to cost me?" He liked to get rid of the business part up front.

She ran her eyes over his well-worn jeans and shirt, "A few hours of your time and the price of a room. Or would you prefer the park?" She was cocking that eyebrow at him again and he nearly lost control. Who knew such a simple gesture could be so damned sexy."

The mere thought of taking this woman in the park nearly made him cream his jeans. "Right this way," he said indicating the stairs at the back of the room with a sweep of his arm. *Oh yeah!* He was salivating as he watched her walk away. His imagination had come nowhere near the perfection as her pants caressed her cheeks with each step she took.

They didn't make it to the first landing before Luke reached out and caught one of those gently swaying cheeks in one large hand. She faltered as electricity shot between them. The scent of her need rose in the air between them, and Luke inhaled deeply letting it fuel his own need.

She smelled like heather and sunshine, and sex. Hot—creamy—sex. He growled low in his throat and gently squeezed the cheek resting in the palm of his hand. "Move," he growled. "Unless you want me to take you right here."

Jade's amber eyes sparkled with mischief and something that made his pants tighten even more. She slowly licked her top lip, and practically purred. "Where to?"

Luke swallowed, swept her up into his arms, and ran up the remaining stairs to his room. She weighed no more than a child as she nuzzled his neck. He had no problem holding her while he retrieved his key from his pocket, and unlocked the door.

Luke tossed the key on the only table, and kicked the door shut with his foot. He didn't need to check. It was the type of door that was always locked.

Jade chose that moment to lick the vein on the side of his neck. Luke was so distracted he stumbled. Jade's feet landed on the floor between them with a small thud when he reached out to balance himself against the wall, but he didn't loosen his grip. The room was filled with the scent of humour, lust, wolf, and *cat!*

Luke spun Jade around so that she was against the door, thereby putting himself between her and the unseen threat. He leaned down and nuzzled her neck, letting his own senses reach around the room. They were alone.

Definitely alone.

He sniffed, and tasted the air. Heather and sunshine, musk, wolf. The scent of the cat had already faded. Luke forced himself to relax. The scent of the cat bothered him, but he would worry about that later. *Much later.* Right now he had much more important things on his mind. *Besides, there's no immediate danger.* He nibbled the neck he was nuzzling.

Her quiet laughter reminded him of bells tinkling in the wind. *"Watch the fangs, wolf."* Luke froze, his teeth gently scraping the pretty neck. *"I don't want to kill you."* The voice was tinged with humour, but the words were very serious-- and inside his head.

"Who are you?" He growled the words with his mind, but there was no answer. *Was his conscience a woman?* The little voice in his head wasn't usually female. Besides, he knew the law as well as he knew his own name. If he did bite the woman, he would be signing his own death warrant. There were only two times that were even remotely acceptable when it came to biting a human. Self-defence; and your life better be in immediate danger. He inhaled the scent of the woman in his arms. No danger there. *Unless she's planning to screw my brains out and I wouldn't fight that.*

The only other time it was acceptable to bite a human, was if the human happened to be your mate. It wasn't that rare of an occurrence either. With so few female werewolves in the world, more and more males were finding their mates in the human population; More of the females as well. As her scent surrounded him, Luke shuddered. *Now that might be a fate worse than death.* He had no intention of ever mating. Once, long ago, he had thought it an option, but her betrayal and the consequent death of his parents and most of his people had abused him of that notion.

There were times when he watched his friends with their children that he wondered what it would be like to be a father. If he were to choose a mate amongst the lycan population then their offspring would be lycan. However, if he found his mate amongst the human population their offspring would only have the lycan gene. The gene would be passed down from generation to generation, but only if it was dominant would the young actually become lycan. There were times when the gene would lay dormant for centuries in a family before one would be born with the dominant gene.

There was no worry that Luke would ever choose a human mate--again. You couldn't guarantee how a human would react. It was better just to use them for sex, and leave. All offspring had to be monitored for the gene, and those carrying it had to be watched for signs of turning. Luke had been on his way home after checking on the birth of a latent lycan when he decided to spend the night in the city. Several members of his pack had once been humans. But they had all been exceptional, and they had all been psychic. Being psychic seemed to make it easier for them to accept the lycan gene and survive the change.

Jade shifted slightly drawing Luke's attention. He welcomed the distraction from his thoughts. "Having second thoughts?" Her voice was a smoky purr.

Luke's lust rose at the tone. "Second. Third. What's it matter. They are all about you." He began opening the small round buttons on her blouse, and growled when his large hands fumbled. When she laughed, he grasped the sides of the blouse, and yanked. The frustrating buttons flew everywhere.

Jade laughed, and put her hands in his dark hair, standing on her tiptoes she reached up to capture his mouth with hers. Power sparked between them. Luke groaned. *Maybe she was going to be dangerous to his health. She was definitely dangerous to his good sense.* Cupping the cheeks of her ass in his large hands he lifted until she wrapped her legs around his waist. She didn't release his mouth. Her smaller tongue slid between his lips to explore his sharp, even teeth.

Luke moaned. "You're killing me." Jade loosened her hold on him so he could pull her blouse off her arms, to discard it by the door. Jade reached under Luke's shirt to caress the rock hard abs beneath. Luke pinned her between himself and the door as she pulled the shirt over his head, and tossed it beside her own.

Jade leaned into him, and with the tip of her tongue flicked one taut nipple. Luke's growl rumbled deep in his chest, and he grabbed her ass as he spun her away from the door. Jade laughed, and caught his shoulders to keep from falling backwards. He took a couple of long strides and they fell on the bed together.

The room was small. There was a table, two chairs, and a bed. A sliding glass door led to a small balcony, and another small door led to the bathroom. Neither of them cared about the room. The bed was the only thing they were interested in, and it was huge.

Luke stood up, not once taking his eyes from the woman on the bed as he undid the buttons on his jeans, and slowly slid them over his hips and down his muscled legs. He wasn't wearing any underwear. Jade leaned on her elbows staring, as his erection sprang free of the confines of his pants. She slowly ran her tongue over her lips, and his erection grew.

The scent of their arousal filled the room. The power sparking from her eyes should have concerned Luke; instead it turned him on more. He kicked his shoes off, and his pants followed. He reached down and tore his socks off. He hated wearing them anyway. He leaned towards Jade. "Fairs fair," he said, and caught one taut nipple between his teeth.

Jade moaned with pleasure as he laved the nipple, and then moved to worship the other. While he was busy suckling, his hands were busy with her pants. He loosened them, and slid them down over her hips. Releasing her nipples he leaned back, and slowly slid her pants down her long legs, and tossed them away.

It was Luke's turn to stare. His eyes glazed with lust, and he licked his lips in anticipation. She lay before him with her legs slightly splayed--an offering to the gods. "God you are beautiful." Her naked skin glowed with power, and her amber eyes swirled with mystery. *What are you?* he wondered. *Not lycan. I'd know if you were lycan.*

She cocked her eyebrow, and he groaned. "Do you know what you do to me when you look at me like that?" He dropped to his knees beside the bed and pulled her so she was hanging off the edge. "I can't wait to taste you." He lifted her legs exposing her most vulnerable self to his hot gaze. Then ever so slowly he leaned over, and nibbled her knee. His beard scratched her skin, and the friction nearly drove her insane. He alternated sides, taking his time. When his mouth finally reached her creamy center Jade was writhing with pleasure.

Luke inhaled deeply. "Oh, yeah."

"Oh! My! God!" Jade screamed the words as he slid his tongue deep inside her honeyed core. Luke savoured every drop of her orgasm. She was still trembling when he slid first one, and then a second finger deep inside. "You are so tight. So hot."

Luke was surprised at how tight she was. And pleased. Her fingers tangled in his dark hair. With her head thrown back against the sheets she rode his pumping fingers to another climax. Luke removed his fingers, and slowly licked them clean. Her eyes shone as she watched him. Her breath came in short, harsh bursts. God. He hadn't enjoyed a woman like this in a very long time. *Too long.*

He leaned forward and slowly licked her. She moaned and arched towards his mouth. Slowly he worked his way up her body. Nibbling and licking as he went, spending long moments to worship each nipple. When he slid his aching shaft into her hot creamy core she was already writhing in the throes of another climax. Luke covered her mouth with his, swallowing her mindless screams as he shattered with his own mind bending climax.

Mine!

The word roared in his head.

Chapter Nine

There were hands everywhere. Warm, firm hands. They stroked her breasts, bringing her nipples to firm peaks. A hand traveled down the outside of her leg, leaving a burning trail through the thin material of her jeans. It moved to the inside of her leg, and hot liquid pooled at her center.

Slowly, too slowly to her way of thinking, his hand traveled along the inside of her leg until it reached its destination. She was burning for his touch. It was both exciting and frightening. Never before had anyone touched her like this.

His hand was rough as he rubbed it against her jeans.

She opened her mouth to tell him to stop. To quit teasing her, before the flames consumed her.

No sound came.

Gemma jerked to a sitting position. Sweat trickled between her breasts. Her heart pounded. Slowly her eyes adjusted to the dark. She took a deep, cleansing breath. Relief flooded through her.

It was just a dream, brought on by the coming of the full moon, or a nightmare, depending on how you looked at it.

She was safe in her own room, in her own bed. Alone. She listened to the familiar sounds of the night, and slowly relaxed. A glance at the bedside clock told her it was four a.m. No sense trying to get back to sleep. She had to get up in an hour anyway.

She jumped out of bed and headed for the bathroom. A hot shower was the ticket. Gemma took two steps and a wave of dizziness enveloped her. She had to grab the dresser to keep herself from falling to the floor.

What was wrong with her?

Gemma was really worried now. She couldn't remember being sick a single day in her life, and now it seemed she was sick every day. Something was definitely wrong.

The dizziness passed. She clutched her stomach and ran for the toilet. Twenty minutes later she was still leaning into the bowl. The contents of her evening meal floated in the water, undigested. Dry heaves wracked her bruised body. One more, long tremor shook her, and then they stopped. Gemma waited several more minutes before carefully climbing to her feet. Maybe if she moved very, very, slowly she could make it the four steps to the shower.

The stinging spray of icy water on her skin helped her feel better. It always did.

What had she done? For days now she had wracked her brains, and still hadn't come up with an answer. The last time she could remember feeling good was the day before she went to the bar with Sara.

Stupid. Stupid. Stupid.

She knew the dangers of drinking. Not just the usual ones, either. Losing control for her kind meant the possibility of exposure. Or worse.

Why had she done it?

What had she done?

If only she could remember. She was sure that if she could remember what had happened the night she went to the bar, then everything would be okay. It would have to be.

She had a vague recollection of some guy. Who was he? She tried to focus on his image. She tried to get a good look at his face. She pressed the heels of her hands to her temples, and tried to still the sudden pain.

Damn! Every time she was almost there. Every time she could just about see his face, this happened.

She looked at the clock. Great! It was five thirty. If she didn't hurry she was going to be late, and it wasn't like her to be late. If she was late today, Elizabeth would know something was wrong; if she didn't already.

Elizabeth was an alpha female, as well as being a healer, and had the gift of precognition. Gemma knew she should go to her.

She was afraid.

What if she'd done something bad? What if she'd broken one of their laws? Uncle Luke would have to punish her. He'd had to punish Gheorgès when he'd broken their laws. Gemma hadn't actually met Gheorgès. He had *died* a long time before she was born, but she knew the story. As much as Uncle Luke loved her, if she broke their laws she *would* be punished. As Alpha of the pack he would have no choice, and as a temporary member of his pack she was under his domain. Even her parents wouldn't be able to save her if she broke their laws.

When Gemma arrived at The Wolf Center, affectionately known by the pack as 'The Den', at six o'clock Elizabeth was already there. Gemma had known, deep down, that she would be. Whenever Uncle Luke was away, Elizabeth took control. On the edge of the town of Willow Bend, The Den consisted of a museum of the area wildlife and a research facility for the study of wolves. It was also a veterinary training hospital, and the reason Gemma was there. Gemma was studying to be a doctor, and because of the physical nature of lycans she also needed training in veterinary studies. To pay for that training she worked as a guide at

The Den, amongst other things, whenever she wasn't actually working with Elizabeth..

"Morning, Elizabeth." Gemma forced herself to act normal. At least as normal as possible with her head pounding and her heart racing.

Elizabeth's dark eyes searched Gemma's face carefully. Then they scanned her from head to toe, searching. On the way back up they stayed on her stomach for several seconds. Gamma wanted to squirm. She tried to force herself to stand still. Her hand had a mind of its own. It strayed to her bangs and shoved them back. They fell forward.

Elizabeth's eyes strayed to the movement. She grinned. It was a grin full of knowledge and secrets. "Good morning, child," she finally said. "I'll be glad when your hair gets back to normal."

Secretly, Gemma agreed. She had thought about coloring her hair, again, but when she'd mixed the dye, the smell had made her throw up. She was glad she hadn't let Sara convince her to use a permanent color. This should wash out completely in another week or so. Until then, she would have to put up with streaks of blonde and brown. The bangs, however, would take much longer to grow back to normal.

She chose to ignore Elizabeth's comment. "Have you been here long?" Gemma asked instead.

"Depends what you call long." Elizabeth chuckled and winked at Gemma, in a rare show of humour. "A century or two isn't all that long."

Gemma couldn't help herself. She smiled, and it felt good.

"Been here all night," Elizabeth continued. "I went running last night. Stopped in by your place but you were sleeping." Again with that searching look. "Funny thing, though," Elizabeth said. "It doesn't look like you slept much at all. Are you okay?"

"I'm fine," Gemma said quickly. Maybe a little too quickly because Elizabeth gave her the once over again. "I just didn't sleep well."

"Good to know." Elizabeth tilted her head to one side and seemed to be listening to something, or someone. Then she straightened and stared straight through Gemma. "You suppose to go out overnight"?

Gemma nodded. What was Elizabeth up to? She knew well enough that Gemma had an overnight. Elizabeth knew everything that happened, not only at The Den, but in the entire town.

"Actually..." Gemma pushed her bangs back, and then puffed at them once when they fell back in place. She glanced meaningfully at the office door. Just out of reach behind Elizabeth. "... We are heading out to Wolf Lake Falls. So if you'll excuse me, I have to check on the supplies." Wolf Lake didn't actually have a waterfall, just a series of three sets of rapids in a row. However, the sound of the rushing water, coupled with the calm waters of the lake at the bottom, made it a favourite spot to take the overnight campers. And it was the only site with a cabin for the off season.

Gemma tried to slip past Elizabeth, but her small hand caught her arm. "Don't go."

Gemma spun back to face Elizabeth. "What is it?" she asked, suddenly worried. "Are you alright?" To her, Elizabeth looked the same as she always did. Her hair was neatly plaited to her waist. Her clothes were immaculate. Her dark eyes glittered with life and laughter. They looked like they were laughing at Gemma right now.

Then they changed; became serious. "*I* am fine, child," she said.

"Then what?" Gemma knew she sounded testy. She was testy.

"*Don't* go to Wolf Lake Falls."

Gemma chewed on her bottom lip, thoughtfully, and looked at the older woman. What was going on? Don't go to

Wolf Lake Falls? She and George always took the overnight to Wolf Lake Falls. Especially during a full moon, and tonight was the beginning of the cycle. "Is something wrong?"

"Sara can go." Elizabeth's tone was clipped.

"No way!" Gemma shook the hand off her arm. "Are you nuts?" Oh crap! What's gotten into her lately? Nobody. Absolutely nobody argued with Elizabeth. Except maybe Uncle Luke.

Elizabeth drew herself to her full five feet three inches and looked Gemma in the eye. Despite her smaller size she gave the impression of towering over Gemma. "Are you challenging me?"

Gemma glared down at the smaller woman. She held her eyes for about two seconds, and then dropped hers to the floor. She began worrying at an imaginary spot on the pristine floor with her right toe. "No, Ma'am," she finally mumbled.

"I didn't think so." Elizabeth turned and headed for the office. She stopped abruptly and Gemma, who had been following meekly behind, nearly bumped into her. "Call Sara. She'll need to pack."

"Yes, Elizabeth." Gemma hated the way she squirmed before the woman's watchful eyes. One day, she told herself, she would stand up to Elizabeth. One day. Just not today.

Elizabeth reached out and patted Gemma's shoulder. Gemma looked up and saw compassion in the older woman's eyes. "It'll be all right, child," she told her. "Things have a way of working out for the best."

Elizabeth turned then and entered Luke's office without saying another word.

Gemma went behind the small desk in the reception area. She dialled the familiar number, and while the phone rang she worried about Sara's reaction. This was terrible. Just yesterday Sara had threatened to claw Georges' eyes out; all because George had made her feel like a child in front of Mark. Gemma was afraid to leave the two of them alone.

Sure, there would be a dozen other people with them, but Gemma knew George. He wouldn't let the presence of anyone keep him from what he wanted.

And he wanted Sara.

Gemma wasn't blind. She could see it in the way he watched her. She was surprised Sara couldn't see it. Maybe Sara did see it, and just didn't care. She treated him like a brother, which seemed to infuriate George. It really wasn't a good idea to put those two together for the night. Especially with the moon rising. Gemma prayed that without her calming presence, George would be able to control his wilder instincts.

Gemma watched with trepidation as the group climbed into the center's two Hummers and drove off. After her initial tirade, Sara had accepted the fact that she, not Gemma, would be spending the night with George.

"He better not try and tell me what to do?" Sara had stomped around, putting supplies in the packs. Occasionally she glared at George, where he lounged insolently against the doorframe. "I don't know why you can't go. You're used to handling this beast."

"Afraid you can't handle it?" George taunted. He laughed when Sara threw a can of beans at him. "Maybe it's me you're afraid of." He sauntered out the door, a self-satisfied grin on his handsome face, before Sara could reply.

Hours later, Gemma locked the office and climbed into her own jeep. Her stomach grumbled. She thought about going to the Hub for dinner. She hadn't seen Tony for a while. Tony was in his late twenties, but most of the time he acted like a teenager. His dad spoiled him rotten, probably because his mother died during childbirth, but he was always looking for a party and always a lot of fun.

Gemma decided what she really wanted was something fresh. To tell the truth, the idea of anything cooked made her stomach queasy. She honked as she drove past the diner. By the time she pulled in front of her own cabin a plan had formulated.

She would go for a hunt. Nothing big. Just a rabbit. Or maybe a beaver. Then she could run down to Wolf Lake Falls and howl at the full moon. Of course George would know it was her. She just wished she could see the look on the other's faces. If she timed it just right, Sara would be right in the middle of her story when they heard her.

This was going to be fun.

Gemma sniffed the air. She was alone. She knew she would be, but the need to be sure had been drilled into her at a very early age.

She hurried into the house and removed her clothes. Moonlight bathed her pale skin when she left the cabin, and the early spring air brought goose bumps to the surface, but she knew she would be warm enough once the change took effect. She didn't bother to lock the door. The pack owned over one thousand acres of private forest and mountains, not including what they owned in town, and her cabin was built on these acres.

Gemma walked the ten feet to the edge of the clearing. The moon beckoned. Its brilliant rays teased and enticed. She was a child again, feeling its pull for the first time. Tonight she would be free and let the moon work its magic.

She knelt. Catching her medallion between her thumb and forefinger she began to gently rub it. Gemma had always been able to control the change at will. It was one of the reasons that she and George worked the overnights. She envisioned the wolf in her head. Concentrated on the vision. A warm tingling began in her fingers. It traveled up her arms. It spread to her legs. She could feel something crawling beneath her skin. The transformation had begun. Hot, piercing pain spread through her veins. A million needles broke through her skin, as fur spread over her body. She could hear and feel her bones breaking. Gemma screamed. She let go of the medallion and wrapped her arms around herself. She rolled to the ground, murmuring a prayer as darkness stole over her.

Chapter Ten

David Woods stared at the sandwich that had just been delivered. White-hot anger slashed through his veins and throbbed at his temples. Everything around him turned red. He had an almost overwhelming urge to march down to the deli and rip someone's throat out. David tore the top layer of bread off, and ripped out the offending slice of ham. He threw it against the door. How long has he been getting his dinner from there? Five years? Moreover, not once had he *ever* bought any kind of meat.

He looked at the slimy trail down the door and the meat on the floor. Damn! Why had he done that?

David took several, deep, calming breaths. He grabbed a paper towel, and walked towards the door. He had better get this mess cleaned up. Near the door he froze, and sniffed the air. *What was that smell?* He cocked his head sideways and looked at the meat, a puzzled expression on his face. He jerked his hand down and picked up the offending slice of meat. The thought of eating it made his stomach churn. The smell made his mouth water.

He shoved the ham into his mouth and swallowed.

David Woods tore the door open. He loped down the hall and out of the building.

A rush of air hit him. David stopped. What was he doing out here? He couldn't just leave. His equipment was on the counter. There were vials of blood still waiting to be examined. His blood was in one of those vials. David had drawn it that morning. He was going to find out what was wrong with him, one way or the other. It was the perfect opportunity. The other research assistant had the week off, and Dr. Madison was at a fundraiser. He had even labelled the container 'specimen three,' just in case someone came in. It didn't happen often. Nevertheless, even Dr. Madison couldn't keep the investors from making unexpected appearances. Dr. Madison might even show up after the fundraiser to check on things. He was so paranoid about his research that even David, who had been working with him for five years, wasn't allowed in the underground labs. David wondered, not for the first time, what exactly the doctor was doing down there. There were plenty of rumours—some even hinted at the doctor's deeds being illegal. David knew it had something to do with DNA manipulation, and the government was financing the whole thing. They were merging the genes of one animal with the genes of another, in the hopes of developing a new gene therapy as a cure for cancer. So far they hadn't been successful.

David wondered, briefly, if he had closed the door. He knew he hadn't locked it.

The spicy aroma of sizzling sausages caught his attention. Hunger was a machete slicing at his insides. He forgot about the door, and everything else, as he turned towards the tantalizing aroma of sausage, and started to jog.

He bought two. He didn't bother with mustard or onions. He threw the dry buns to a flock of squawking gulls, then wolfed down the meat.

The breeze ruffled his hair. He sniffed again. His brain took a while to sort through the myriad smells. The overpowering lavender scent of cheap perfume reminded him of the woman who had raised him. How he hated that smell. Had the stench of rotting fruit and vegetables from the dumpster behind a nearby restaurant always been this strong? Why hadn't he noticed it before? The sweet odour of freshly mowed grass; these and much, much more traveled on the breeze.

His head was splitting. David reached into the pocket of his lab coat and pulled out a bottle of pills. He shook two into his hand. He looked at them, wondering briefly where they had come from. He shrugged and popped them into his mouth. The pills began to work immediately. The tension left his body. His headache began to ease. He was floating.

Was this how the girls felt? Had they been floating on a cloud? Or had they felt like they were drowning—able to see the surface just above them, yet unable to reach it. He knew how he had felt. Powerful. Invincible. In control.

Not like in school.

In school he had been a geek. His ears had been too big. His eyes had been enormous, behind his Coke-bottle glasses. Too tall ... too skinny... too smart. He had shown them. He'd worked hard, gotten excellent grades, and continued his education. He had worked out at the gym three times a week – he still did. When he was in his first year of University he had laser surgery. It had been while he was in university that he had worked for the pharmaceutical company. That's where he had learned how to manufacture his own special party favours.

Like the one he'd slipped *her*.

He should go home to bed. That's what he should do. If he had some decent sleep he would feel better. Lack of sleep had to be responsible for his headaches.

Something crawled along his arm, just under his skin.

He thought about his blood back at the lab waiting to be tested. What if there was something wrong with him? What would he do? He couldn't worry about that until he knew for sure. He couldn't panic. When *she* bit him he'd panicked.

His fingers strayed to his shoulder and he gently massaged it. He rolled his shoulder. There was no pain. It was more like a tingling, or burning sensation, and it was in all his limbs, not just his shoulder. There wasn't a mark on his shoulder where she had bitten him. Looking at it, you couldn't tell she had even broken the skin. Thinking back, David wasn't sure it had even hurt at the time, but the blood had been everywhere, and there had been so much of it.

He had been shocked when she'd bitten him. She shouldn't have been able to move.

She hadn't been moving when he'd left her in the clearing.

David had panicked. He admitted it now. He could still feel his fingers closing around her throat. His thumbs slowly applying pressure, his arms beginning to tingle. It had been that sudden jolt, and the fire bursting through his thumb that had snapped him out of it. He'd jumped back and stared at the medallion lying against her pale skin. A wolf had stared back at him. Its eyes glowed red.

Frowning, he looked at his thumb and the image of that same wolf stared back at him. Funny it didn't hurt. A tattoo burned into the skin like that should hurt. It seemed more distinct today. Clearer. Every time he looked at it his thoughts turned to *her*.

His stomach rumbled, and David quickened his pace. He decided to stop at the grocery store on his way home. All he had in the fridge was the makings of a salad. He was pretty sure that wasn't going to be enough. What he really wanted was a nice, juicy steak.

Chapter Eleven

The park was beautiful. The full moon glistened off the tranquil surface of the fishpond. Eden in the middle of the city. Maggie couldn't see it for the tears in her eyes but she knew it was there. She knew this park as well as she knew the back of her hand. She had spent many hours here, day and night, by herself, thinking; Away from everyone and everything.

Damn them anyway. She slapped at her eyes with the back of her hand and kept walking. Who did they think they were? Brenda was supposed to be her very best friend. Just last week Jason had been trying his best to get into *her* pants.

"Come on, baby," he'd said. "If you love me you'll do it." But she hadn't and now he was '*doing it*' with Brenda. Well damn him. Damn Brenda too. She didn't need them. She didn't need anyone.

The gentle swaying of the swings in the breeze drew her and she sat down. She couldn't go home. She was supposed to be at Brenda's all night. She wasn't going back to the party. Besides, if she showed up crying her Mom would want to know what happened. She couldn't tell her Mom she'd walked in on Jason and Brenda in bed. Her Mom would call Brenda's Mom and all hell would break loose.

Maybe she *should* tell her Mom what happened. Why should she care if Brenda got in trouble? It was obvious Brenda didn't care about her.

Then again, that was the trouble. She did care what happened to Brenda. Brenda *was* her very best friend. She had been her best friend since kindergarten. They spent every weekend at each other's houses. She was the sister Maggie didn't have. Hell, their families vacationed together. You couldn't throw that away because of one stupid night.

What were they thinking anyway? They had to know she would catch them. Brenda was her best friend. What kind of a friend made out with your boy friend?

The moon slipped behind a cloud, blocking out the light. A sudden shiver passed through her and she pulled her jacket closed. The heavy scent of lilacs hung in the air. She inhaled their sweet fragrance. Lilacs were her favourite. They shouted spring better than anything else. She loved the way they smelled. She loved the solitude of the park at night. No laughing, pushy kids. No barking dogs.

No teenage boy making out with his girlfriend's best friend.

The usually calming atmosphere of the park at night did nothing for her. Not even the heady odour of her favourite flowers could calm her. She grabbed the ropes of the swing and walked back as far as she could. She jumped on the wooden slat, kicked her feet out in front of her, and soared. She pumped harder and harder, rising higher and higher. The chill air felt good against her face. Her tear stained cheeks dried and she began to relax.
*****

The wolf stepped on a twig. It snapped. The sound echoed in the quiet night. The Beast froze. Then slowly it moved forward. Its prey was straight ahead. It sniffed, catching the scent of the female, mingled with the strong scent of flowers. She was alone. The wolf could smell ... Anger. It hesitated. A voice inside its head told it to go back; to leave this place and this human.

Hunger drove it forward.

It no longer stayed in the shadows. There was no need. Clouds covered the moon. The night was dark. If the clouds moved and the human looked this way she wouldn't see it. The wolf blended into the night. She wouldn't see it until it wanted her to.

The darkness didn't impede it. It had excellent night vision. The breeze carried her scent. It was intoxicating. She was young and vulnerable. Her blood called to the wolf.

Its stomach rumbled. It growled, deep in its throat.

She looked in its direction. She jammed her feet on the ground to stop the motion of the swing and nearly fell on her face.

The taste of fear danced on the breeze. The wolf's ears leaned back. The tip of its tail began to twitch. It could smell her blood rushing through her veins. The wolf ran its tongue over its canines in a vaguely human gesture. The moon broke free from the clouds. The girl began to run.

Chapter Twelve

Gemma opened her eyes. Cautiously! Everything was dark. It was like trying to look through heavy gauze. Hunger was a living thing, gnawing at the edges of her sanity. Her body was agony and the fear was paralyzing.

Was she dead? Was this what it was like when you died? Blind, in utter agony, and terrified to move. If so, then she really didn't want to be dead. Not that she wanted to be dead if it were all fairy clouds and bliss. She had barely started living. She had the whole world to explore. No. She couldn't be dead.

If not dead, then what was wrong with her? Think. Come on, Gemma. Think.

Thinking wasn't easy with that incessant fear trying to take control. She had to calm down and think. *Take a deep breath and relax. Now, isn't that better?* A little calmer. If only her heart would quit racing. This was crazy. Now she was talking to herself. She hadn't done that since the first change. Back then she had talked to her wolf-self like it was another being, not a part of her, until she found the path between her two selves that helped to keep her sane. Without it, she might have lost herself completely to the wolf and the bloodlust. She couldn't let that happen, ever. In the meantime, she had to find out exactly where she was.

Take a deep breath. What do you smell?

Several images rushed through her mind ... grass ... pine trees ... the carcass of a decaying squirrel. This was how the wolf communicated, with pictures instead of words. These pictures didn't really help her. There were pine trees, grass and squirrels at home, and Gemma knew, deep down, that she wasn't at home.

A steady creaking noise intruded on her thoughts. A wave of dizziness swept over her at the suddenness of visions flashing before her eyes. Grass ... trees ... grass. *Stop waving your head around and let me see what's going on.*

The swaying stopped as suddenly as it began. Gemma took the opportunity to look for something familiar. She was lying on a bed of pine needles, almost completely hidden behind the long branches of a very old pine. She could see a cement wall to her left, and the grass to her right was even and tidy. A blur of movement brought a young girl on a swing into focus.

The wolf rose from its bed of needles and moved silently to the edge of the tree. Its eyes were steady on the girl. Hunger pricked its stomach. A sense of unease enveloped Gemma. The wolf should be a part of her, not a separate entity. Without her there could be no wolf.

The wolf didn't seem to realize this. It ignored Gemma and slunk forward.

What are you doing? We shouldn't be here. We need to go back to the cabin. There she would be safe in her own secure little world, not roaming around a strange park, stalking a human. *Stop!*

The wolf hesitated. A twig snapped beneath its paw. The creaking of the swing stopped. The wolf looked directly at the girl. The fear shining in her eyes was a beacon. The girl glanced somewhere to the right of them. The wolf's ears bent back and its tail began to slowly wag. The sour scent of her fear was intoxicating, urging them on. The wolf's heart pumped with excitement. The girl made her decision, turned and ran towards the far gate.

Gemma enjoyed a good chase as much as the next wolf. The adrenaline rush while hunting was incomparable, and today was no different. Gemma found herself caught in the excitement of the pounding feet, with the wind in her face, and she forgot everything else.

The wolf pounced. Its teeth closed over the girl's leg, bringing her to the ground. As realization dawned, Gemma's scream echoed across two minds. The wolf released the girl and slunk back towards the safety of the pines.

With the wolf under control, Gemma let her guard down. Once again darkness swept over Gemma, this time like a welcome blanket.

Chapter Thirteen

Amber eyes flew open.

Something was out there.

Jade was wide-awake. She snuggled against the man laying behind her, and inhaled deeply. Musky pine and campfire invaded her senses, making her tingle all the way to her toes. Jade longed to roll over and wake him with a kiss. The mere thought of his hands on her skin made her burn. Just reach up and kiss him. That's all she had to do and the pleasure would begin again. Jade allowed herself a few more seconds of fantasy before she sighed, and careful not to wake him, slid out from beneath his arm.

Their clothing was strewn around the room. Her silk blouse was crumpled with several buttons missing. Her slacks were in the same condition. A testimonial to their impatience the night before. Jade pulled on the clothes leaving the shirt to hang open.

Jade snatched a handful of grapes from the fruit bowl on the table, and shoved them in her mouth. Her mind wandered to the man in the bed. He was strong, powerful, and unnaturally quiet. Just being with him seemed to block out the city, and had done more to restore her than forty-eight hours of sleep would have. It was a good thing she didn't know how to find him again. If she did, she might be tempted to call him up and say, 'Hey, remember me? We took a tumble a few nights ago. How about a rematch?' Or, "I have an itch and was wondering if you'd like to meet me somewhere and scratch it?' No. It was just as well she didn't know his name. Less chance she would do something really stupid. *Let's not forget the fact that he is a wolf.*

Jade grabbed another handful of grapes, popped some in her mouth, opened the sliding-glass door and stepped onto the balcony. The sky was beginning to lighten. The street outside was empty, but that wouldn't last long. Lights were already coming on in the surrounding neighbourhood. Soon the street would be busy. Jade took advantage of the peacefulness and reached out with her senses. The sound of running water came from a house at the end of the block. There was fresh brewed coffee somewhere to the east. Her stomach rumbled. She bit into another grape, allowing the juice to trickle down her throat before swallowing. What she really wanted was a nice, juicy burger. The whistle of a kettle blew two blocks over. She ignored it and kept searching, sweeping the area in an ever growing circle.

Behind her the bed creaked. Once again musky pine and campfire filled her senses. Memories of the previous night brought a smile, and a warm feeling deep inside. She felt strong arms circling her and pulling her close. *He* was so close, maybe a little too close. Jade forced his image into a secret place, to be brought out and savoured later, and focused on her search.

There was something going on just to the east. Sirens and men shouting.

Jade popped the remaining grapes into her mouth, and climbed onto the railing, shifting as she went. Seconds later a large, white owl flew towards the rising sun. Several minutes later she saw the flashing lights. The smell of blood beckoned.

Jade flew on silent wings, searching the ground. There were several police cars already on the scene. An ambulance was parked nearby. A couple of officers were busy placing police tape around the park. Others were trying to keep the inevitable reporters back. Several more officers were searching the area. Jade had the advantage of seeing the entire scene at once.

Her sharp eyesight easily found where the predator had lain in wait. The grass was matted. There were several blurred tracks in the dirt. Jade recognized the scent of wolf. It took longer to find the path the girl had taken. There was so much blood.

Jade forced her owl-self to concentrate on the scene below. Faint footprints showed the path the prey had taken. They entered the park through the main gate, and then passed the pond and the formal garden. The tracks had been taking a straight line towards the creek, and a footbridge leading to a small townhouse complex, when they had veered towards the swings.

Landing in a nearby tree, Jade scanned the prints at the base of the swing to the body laying several yards away. The scent of fresh meat called to the predator in her. Her stomach muscles twisted and clenched. A small mouse skittered through the pine needles beneath a row of trees. The owl took to the sky.

Nobody noticed the blue shimmering light between the ambulance and a news van. If anyone looked they would see an ordinary woman, wearing a beige cable knit sweater, comfortable blue jeans, and plain sneakers. A wave of dizziness washed over her and Jade caught the side of the van to steady herself. Her stomach twisted and she clenched her teeth to keep from crying out. Clothing was relatively simple but even that took energy. She had to eat. The mouse had simply been a tease.

This needed to be done. Jade pushed away from the van and walked towards the park. They were getting ready to move the body. Food would have to wait.

"Excuse me, Miss." She stopped when a hand clasped her shoulder. "No press this side of the line."

Jade turned and gave the officer one of her most dazzling smiles. She reached into her back pocket and appeared to pull out a small plastic card. She showed it to the officer. "Not press," she said. "Jade Caer. I'm with O'Connell Search and Rescue, out of New York I've been tracking a runaway."

The officer looked long and hard at the card. Then he looked at Jade. "You're a long way from home." He shook his head slightly, and looked at the card again before making his decision. "Wait here a minute, Miss." He walked over to a nearby police van and spoke to another officer. He returned carrying a small plastic tag with "Pass" printed on it. He reached forward and clipped the nametag to her sweater. His jaw dropped when the tag fell to the ground.

Jade bent down and picked up the tag before the officer moved. "That's okay." Jade smiled again. "I can do it. Sometimes the pins slip through the threads." She clipped the tag to her sweater, and pointed towards the body bag. "What happened?"

"Dog attack. Poor girl. Tore her up pretty bad."

Jade was already walking towards the body. "Mind if I take a look? Make sure she isn't mine?"

The officer hesitated, and then said. "Sure. Go ahead. Just don't touch anything."

The closer Jade got to the body, the stronger the scent of blood and raw meat. The body was still warm. The girl probably hadn't been dead more than a couple of hours. What had she been doing out here by herself, in the middle of the night? The rotting fungus stench of death was overpowering, making it difficult to pinpoint anything else. Still, there was something, teasingly familiar, that Jade couldn't quite grasp.

Jade knelt beside the body, and gathered enough strength to make herself unnoticeable. Even the officer, who had given her the nametag, forgot about her. If he remembered anything later, it would be talking to a woman, who had left without ever entering the park.

Jade took a deep, calming breath. She really hated this part. She reached under the plastic cover and touched the hand beneath.

The world shimmered and changed.

She was on the swing. Her legs pumping harder and harder as the sweet night air, filled with the heady scent of flowers, washed against her face, drying her tears. She was angry with ... Jason and Brenda.

Jade didn't know why. She didn't need to know why. That wasn't what was important.

A blur of movement near the trees caught her attention. She looked but clouds covered the moon, and the night was dark. Suddenly it was too dark. It was too quiet. Where were the crickets that had been playing their melody just minutes before?

Terror clenched her heart in its tight grip. She jammed her feet to the ground. The momentum of the moving swing threw her forward and she went down on all fours. She struggled to her feet and began to run. The footbridge was close. Her house was just on the other side.

Something was there. In the trees beside the bridge.

She couldn't see it, she couldn't hear it, but she knew it was there. She could feel it.

Her heart was thumping. Her legs burned. Her mouth was dry. Still she ran.

She could hear it now. The pounding of feet running towards her. She glanced towards the sound. She stumbled. She saw teeth, claws and fur hurtling through the air towards her. Fire tore through her right leg. Screams ripped from her throat.

She fell to the ground. The weight of the animal forced her to roll. She beat at it with her hands. It opened its mouth and released its hold on her. Her jaw dropped. Her eyes widened. Relief washed over her like a cool, summer rain easing her burning skin. She couldn't believe her luck. It was slinking back towards the trees. She was going to live.

Her right leg was mangled and useless. She looked around for a stick, or something else to use as a crutch. This part of the park, as usual, was immaculate. There wasn't a stick anywhere within reach. She started to drag herself towards the gate.

Another hundred feet, and she'd be home free. She could see the streetlights. She could hear traffic.

This time the attack came from the left. She hit, pushed and clawed. She was crying so hard now she could barely see. The dog, that's the only thing her brain recognized it as, jumped back. This time it didn't slink away. It stood about five fee away. Its dark eyes never left her face. Saliva and blood dripped from its teeth.

She pushed herself up on her elbows and tried to drag herself to the street. She was so tired. Her once burning skin was icy cold. Her legs were numb.

She was dead before its teeth closed over her throat.

Jade came to with a start. Her own heart was racing and she had to concentrate to slow it down. Her legs were numb. She was almost surprised to see them still attached when she looked down. Jade struggled to a standing position and stomped her feet to get the blood flowing. There was nothing she could do for the girl now, except find her killer.

She let her nose lead her to the tantalizing aroma of fresh brewed coffee and sizzling bacon. After a full-size breakfast, with extra ham and sausage, she hailed a cab and returned to the hotel. On the way she spotted a small butcher shop, and had the cabbie pull over. The store was just opening. There was very little meat on the counter. Jade bought two sirloin-tip steaks and a pork chop. Once again she made the clerk believe she had paid, and he gave her a receipt. She would send him his money, when she returned to her room, along with the money for her breakfast. The cabbie waited while she went up to get some cash from her room.

She ate the pork chop as soon as she got back to the room. Then, after a quick shower, she crawled into bed and fell asleep.

Chapter Fourteen

A scream rent the air. The hairs on the back of his neck stood straight. The quiet night erupted with noise. Lykos rushed out into the village square as the warning bell began to clang. His hair streaming out behind, he ran towards the screaming children. There was fighting everywhere. Men, women and children were being slaughtered. The coppery scent of blood filled his nostrils. Hot blood hit the back of his throat as he bit into an enemy. One sharp claw ripped out another's throat as he snatched his baby sister from beneath a descending blade with the other hand. The sound of sinister laughter made him jerk around just in time to see his mother fall beneath the sweep of a blade. Her head rolled in the dirt to stop at his feet. Her pleading eyes stared up at him. She still held two-year-old Gheorgès clenched tight in her arms as she slowly crumpled to the ground.

"Natasha sends her regards."

Luke jerked to wakefulness. It took a moment for the nightmare to recede, and memories of the night before to surface. He reached for the woman beside him. His hand came back empty.

He was alone. Completely alone.

He listened to the silence of the room and groaned. For one brief moment he thought he had dreamed the whole thing—but the evidence was hard to refute.

Unlike Natasha, She had been here. The scent of heather, fresh-cut grass, and sunshine clung to the room. Her scent. He remembered everything about her. The way she looked. The way she felt. The way she tasted. The way it felt when she tasted him. He inhaled deeply, tasting her again.

Her scent was a part of him.

He'd never forget it.

How had she managed to get up and leave without him waking? He stepped out onto the balcony. The breeze whispered around him, caressing him and teasing him with her presence. She couldn't have gotten far. Quickly he pulled on his clothes and set out to search for her.

He picked up her scent outside the hotel, but it was old. Several hours old.

There was a commotion to the east. Ice ran through his veins and he started running, shifting shape in mid stride. He was close enough to hear snippets of conversation, and heard the words "dog attack." Icy tendrils of fear wrapped their claws around his heart, and squeezed. Death hung heavy in the air, and blood called to the wolf in him. This was no dog attack.

Frustrated, he returned to the hotel and checked out. He got behind the wheel of his silver Jag and left the city.

Chapter Fifteen

The man, if you could still call him a man, didn't know where he was, or who he was. He wasn't even aware that the reason he was cold was that he wasn't wearing any clothes. He was running on pure instinct. His mind had completely shattered by the horror and pain of his bones breaking, and his body turning out of itself to become a wolf. His mind wasn't his own anymore. He only knew that he was cold and hungry. He had to find food and shelter because there was nobody else to do it for him.

Picking his aching body from the ground he ignored the grass and rotting leaves that stuck to his skin, and headed north.

The sudden roar of a car engine had him scrambling back into the trees. His heart beat erratically, and his breath came in short, rapid spurts. It was a long time after the car was gone before the gnawing in his stomach forced him to once again venture from the safety of the trees. Lifting his head, the man sniffed the air. Images fluttered across what was left of his mind.

Food.

Keeping the trees between the road and himself the man began to run.

He could see the house now. It was two-stories with blue siding, white trim, and a small shed to one side. One of the windows on the lower level of the house was open, and this was where the smell was coming from.

The man started to run across the clearing towards the house. A door slammed.

"Danger" flashed across his brain in large red letters. He veered to the right and hunkered down behind the shed. The pounding of his heart was deafening.

A sudden roar made him gasp. A car. It was just a car.

He rested his back against the shed, and waited. Five, ten, fifteen minutes passed. Finally, the man stood. He flexed his legs to relieve the cramped muscles and peeked around the corner of the shed.

The house was quiet. The man circled the house slowly, pausing every few seconds to sniff the air, and listen. Satisfied that the house was empty, he entered through the open window, and found himself in a small kitchen. There was a fridge, a stove, a small half-circle table, and one chair. There was a cup with the remains of cold coffee. Crinkling his nose in distaste, the man ignored the cup and sniffed the grease covered plate beside it, before licking it clean.

He opened the fridge and pulled out a carton of milk. The numbers stamped on the carton meant nothing to him. He tore open the top and lifted the carton to his lips, took a big swallow, and spit it out on the floor. He threw the container across the room. He tore open a package of cold meat that was green around the edges. He shoved it in his mouth and swallowed without chewing. He tore open several more containers of food. Some he sniffed and discarded. Others he shoved in his mouth. His mouth watered when he tore open the fresh, pink ground beef. He devoured half the paper with it, before discarding the rest of the wrapper in the growing pile of debris on the floor.

The gnawing in his stomach appeased, the man went to explore the next room. The heat coming from the woodstove drew him. He lay down, wiggling his body between the wall and the stove, not touching either.

He slept.

Several hours later, the creaking of the door woke him. Startled, he pushed his body farther in behind the stove, making it as small as possible.

He waited for his chance to escape.

When Michael Green came home he didn't notice the naked man crouched behind his woodstove. He was having a bad day so he slammed the door shut behind him, and headed straight for the kitchen to grab a beer. One look at the mess on his kitchen floor and he went ballistic. Shouting and cursing, he stomped back into the living room intending to call the Sheriff's office. The punks that did this were going to pay. He'd make sure of it.

Michael headed for the phone on the wall beside the woodstove, and froze. He couldn't believe his eyes. Crouching there like some wild beast, and stark naked was a stranger.

With his escape route cut off, what was left of David Woods panicked. He leapt from behind the woodstove, knocking Michael to the ground. He sank his teeth into Michael's neck. Hot, spicy blood hit the back of his throat, and he was lost. Without hesitation he clamped his teeth down and tore out the other man's throat. He tore chunks of meat from the corpse, chewing and swallowing, gorging himself until completely sated. Then, leaving the ravaged remains, he climbed back through the kitchen window, and escaped to the woods.

Once again, instinct called him north, towards *her*.

Chapter Sixteen

A large white wolf with silver and gray tips wandered back and forth sniffing the ground, then pointed its nose in the air and sniffed. There was no use. The trail was definitely lost—again. In less time that it took a human to blink, Jade shifted into her human form, bent to tie a loose lace on her hiking shoe, and looked around. Lucky for her she kept not only what she was wearing when she shifted, but also anything that was in her pockets, and on her person. She had no problem conjuring clothing, but she had to carry anything else she needed.

Not many people knew that Willow Bend was the largest werewolf community in Canada. Most people believed that *weres*—men or women able to change into animals— vampires, and other supernatural entities were nothing more than superstition and fairy tales. Stories made up to amuse or frighten. Jade was *Moarté*. It was the duty of the *Moarté* to ensure any threat to their survival was dealt with quickly, and anonymously. There were laws in place to ensure the survival of all races, and when a crime was committed Jade became judge, jury, and executioner. One day, if Jade were lucky enough to become a mother, her own daughter would become *Moarté*, as her mother, and grandmother had before her.

All shape shifters were magic, and with so much magic in the area it wasn't going to be easy pinpointing the source she sought. To make matters worse she was here during the full moon cycle, when magic was at its strongest, and lust was in the air. Plus she had no way of knowing whether she was searching for a wolf or a man.

Jade wasn't a *were*. She was a shape shifter. The wolf was a wolf. The fox was a fox. Jade was everything, and nothing. She could change shape at will. She could command the energies of the universe to do her bidding. She could influence people with the power of her mind. She wasn't required to drink blood to survive. She was in full control of herself, and the things around her.

Except three days a month. For three days a month she had an uncontrollable libido. She prowled for partners like a cat in heat. She despised herself for the way she responded to a stranger's touch—any stranger. She had tried locking herself up for three days, but that was disastrous. Without the sexual release she became an irritable bear. Literally. Three hundred pounds of frustrated bear can do a lot of damage.

So three days a month Jade prowled for sexual release. *Weres* were very sexual creatures, but could become very possessive and that was not something that Jade needed in her life. Normally she would avoid *were* communities during the full moon cycle. Yet here she was—with two nights left and a virtual smorgasbord of partners—and all she could think about was a hot, sexy wolf in another city. That was so scary. She was so the love 'em and leave 'em type. Then again, nobody had made her feel the way her wolf had. Not even Larry. And she had married Larry.

Jade shifted her pack on her shoulders, and headed down Main Street. She passed several stores before spotting the Tourist Information Booth. There was nobody inside, but a huge map, dotted with numbers, covered one entire wall. Below it, the corresponding legend showed the names of businesses and other tourist attractions. She found the number for the Inner Sanctum Bed & Breakfast, and then found the corresponding spot on the map.

Ten minutes later she was climbing stone steps to massive oaken doors.

The Inner Sanctum was a six thousand square foot replica of a fourteenth century Romanian castle, built on a two-acre treed lot between a lake and the mountains. It was popular with humans and nonhumans alike. The stone structure could pass for Dracula's castle, probably why it was almost impossible to get a reservation during the month of October. Jade lifted the brass knocker, but wasn't really surprised when the door swung in on silent hinges, before she could use it. The castle was reputed to be protected by a very powerful witch. The appearance of a tiny lady with her gray hair pulled back in a bun, and a delightful twinkle in her sky blue eyes, was a surprise. So much for hunched back servants and old crones.

The woman grabbed her arm and pulled her inside. "Welcome to The Inner Sanctum, Miss Caer. Come in, come in." She pushed the heavy door and it closed with an ominous click, then turned and headed down the wide hallway. "I knew it was you. Everyone else uses the kitchen door. Or the side door. The front doors are mostly for show, except during the season that is. Tourists love using these big old doors. Makes them feel like royalty or something. We don't get many guests during this time of year though. Not enough snow left for skiing and too cold for camping. You're early. You weren't expected until next week."

The woman stopped suddenly and Jade nearly bumped into her. "Oh my," she said. "I hope you don't think I'm complaining. We love visitors any time."

Jade gave a small laugh. She had never heard anyone talk so fast, and all without a pause. "It's okay, Mrs Gray. I will be quite happy with the kitchen door." Or a convenient window from her room.

The clicking of their shoes on the marble floor echoed loudly, making Jade uncomfortable as they passed another massive door, this one with a suit of armour standing guard on either side.

Mrs Gray indicated the door with a wave of her hand, and kept on walking. "That used to be the Chapel. Folks from all around would come every week to give their thanks. And the weddings. Oh the weddings were beautiful." She sighed wistfully. "We don't have a lot of weddings here since they built the new church in town, so we turned it into a library." They continued walking until Mrs Gray indicated a door on the left, also with its attending armour. "This was the Great Hall where the knights would meet with their king and plan their strategies for war."

Mrs Gray paused for a second, a faraway look in her eye. "It acts as a conference room now. You'd be surprised how many companies actually want to book their conferences in a castle. More than once we've had to send them elsewhere. Not that I'm complaining mind you. Conferences are a real boon to the community."

They continued down the seemingly endless hall, and Mrs Gray kept up a running monologue. "This is the Hall of Knights, fitting I say, what with knights guarding all the doors. I can still hear the echo of their armour clinking as they passed down the hall. Now, the only time we get knights are during the Halloween season when we turn the whole thing into a Castle of Horrors."

The flickering glow of the electric candles lining the hall made their shadows grow and shrink, like a funhouse at an amusement park. *Maybe I can bring Alicia here for Halloween. Who am I kidding? I don't even know what she likes. I'm not even sure she will even speak to me again.*

Forcing her attention back to her surroundings, Jade noticed a slight difference in the position of one of the wallboards. Before she could say anything, Mrs Gray reached up to the wall sconce holding the electric candle for this section and twisted it slightly. The panel slid back into alignment with the rest.

"Secret passage," Mrs Gray said. "They're all over the place. We also have a dungeon in the basement, complete with torture chamber. These are off limits to guests. We wouldn't want anyone to get hurt."

At the far end of the hall was an impressive winding staircase. On either side was a door, also with their guardian knights. Jade glimpsed other doors behind the staircase. Before she had a chance to ask, Mrs Gray explained. "The door on the right leads to the dining area. Dinner will be ready in about half an hour. The one on the left leads to the kitchen. The door to the dungeon is through the kitchen. As I said it's off limits except during the guided tours. The double doors behind the staircase lead to the center courtyard. You're welcome to enjoy it whenever you want. The smaller door beside the courtyard leads to my private quarters but you'll usually find me in the kitchen."

Mrs Gray led the way up the stairs her tongue never pausing. Jade could picture her leading the way, a troop of ghosts and goblins trailing behind as she held them spellbound with tales of days gone by. Just listening to her voice, one could almost see the past come to life. "The castle was built almost three hundred years ago, each stone placed by hand. It took nearly fifty years to complete but it was well worth it. My family has been here since the sixteen hundreds."

On the next floor, Mrs Gray led the way down a narrow passageway. The windows on this side were a little larger than the tiny slits on the outer castle walls, and Jade could see the courtyard below. A sugar maple stood at least a hundred feet high in the center of the courtyard. Jade could see a fire pit and tripod.

Mrs Gray noticed the direction she was looking. "Got twelve quarts this year," she said. "Would have got more, but Peter was here with his three little ones and we made toffee in the snow. The look on their faces when they were pulling that toffee was priceless. Don't worry. We still have plenty for our pancake breakfasts."

Mrs Gray winked at Jade. "There's a sugar bush out back."

They continued to the end of the hall, where Mrs Gray opened the door and motioned for Jade to enter. "This room has a window looking out over the courtyard, as well as one that looks out over the forest. You can see the mountains from the one in your room." She flicked a switch inside the door, and several electric candles around the room flared. The lights flickered like real candles, distorting their shadows as they danced on the walls.

"If there's anything you need I'll be in the kitchen." Mrs Gray spoke while she headed back down the passageway. Suddenly she stopped and turned back. "Oh, if you want to lock the door when you go out there's a key in the drawer beside the bed. We don't usually lock the doors, but most city folk feel the need so we supply a key." With that she turned and hurried off.

Jade tossed her pack on the double bed and flopped down beside it. Kicking off her hiking shoes she leaned back and closed her eyes. She couldn't stop the sudden flow of images fluttering across her eyelids, as she remembered the events of the day. There had been so much blood. First the girl in the park. Then that poor man in the house in the woods. That was the big difference between a vampire kill and a wolf kill. The blood. Jade didn't think she would ever get used to the blood.

Jade had picked up the trail outside the park, after several false starts, and followed it through the city. Although they were generally heading north, the trail zigzagged through the streets before finally leaving the city far behind. Around six o'clock Jade found the spot where the wolf had lain down, and the man had woken. She followed the new trail to the house on the edge of the forest. It was isolated, at least a half-mile from its nearest neighbour, and set back from the highway.

As she approached the house Jade knew she was already too late. The dark cloak of Death hung over the building and the coppery scent of blood assailed her through the open window. Jade had known before she went in that he was no longer in the house. The trail clearly led back into the forest. Jade's stomach knotted. She didn't want to go in the house, but she knew she had to. What if someone were alive? She was already carrying around more than enough guilt for the death of the girl. If only she could control her libido. She could have gone out on patrol, that poor girl might still be alive. Taking a deep breath to help still the erratic beating of her heart, Jade went around to the front of the house, and forced herself to open the door. She didn't worry about leaving fingerprints, or any other evidence. Nobody would ever know she had been there.

It was worse than she feared. Blood splattered the walls, the floor, and even the low ceiling. Jade could do nothing for the man. Dead was dead, and even she couldn't change that. She was just thankful nobody else was in the house.

There hadn't been enough left of the victim to connect with, and for that Jade was thankful. She didn't have to relive this man's death to know she had to find the wolf. Tonight. Before he killed again.

Jade shuddered, gave a little bounce and snuggled into the down comforter, forcing the scene from her mind.

Her stomach grumbled, stirring Jade to action. She entered the adjoining bathroom and quickly cleaned up. Mrs Gray had said dinner was in less than half an hour, and Jade didn't want to miss it—not that she missed many meals. Besides, if she didn't take the time to eat she would be useless tonight.

She had just finished tying her shoes when there was a rap at the door.

"Will you be joining us for dinner, Miss Caer?" Mrs Gray asked through the door.

Jade flung open the door and flashed the woman one of her brightest smiles. "I wouldn't miss it for the world. And please, call me Jade." She followed her hostess down the hallway.

"I hope you like venison. It was Mr Gray's favourite. He sure did love a good roast of venison." Mrs Gray tittered like a schoolgirl. "Tell the truth Mr Gray loved a good roast of anything. He sure liked his food. Oh my! I just thought of something. You're not a vegetarian are you?"

"Me? A vegetarian?" Jade's laughter tinkled. "No way. I love meat." Venison was one of her favourites, along with moose, rabbit, bear, beaver, beef, and chicken. You name it; she liked it. Roasted, baked, or fried, it made her mouth water. It was a good thing she liked it raw too, considering she had never taken the time to learn how to cook.

Jade's step faltered when they reached the dining room and there were two other guests already seated at the table. It was strange she hadn't realized anyone else was in the house. It made her wonder what else she had missed. There were at least a dozen other place settings. "Where are the other guests, Mrs Gray?"

"We're all here, my dear. You can never be sure who will drop in at dinner, and we wouldn't want anyone to feel unwelcome. We always set an extra plate." Or a dozen extra places by the look of it.

Mrs Gray waved her hand towards the table. "Have a seat, Miss Jade. Anywhere at all's fine."

"It's Jade," she told Mrs Gray. She tried to keep her voice stern, but her eyes twinkled. "Just Jade."

Jade chose a seat across the table from the gorgeous woman with ebony tresses and coal-black eyes. Jade felt absolutely drab in her olive-green `Illegal Cargo' pants with their many extra pockets, and her beige fisherman-knit sweater, compared to the other woman's obviously expensive tan slacks and satin shirt. It would be better to sit across from her, than beside her where the difference would be much more obvious.

Jade felt the woman watching her and looked up into— *his eyes.* Jade pushed the idea out of her mind. This was ridiculous. The woman's eyes were as black as coal, while his had been a pale brown, except when they blazed yellow while in the throes of passion. Still, they both had that same, penetrating stare. Jade mentally gave herself a shake. She was acting like a schoolgirl with her first crush. Sure he was the sexiest, the most virile male she had been with in decades, but that was no excuse for allowing him to pop into her head whenever he chose.

The other occupant at the table rose from his chair at the end of the table, and stretched his hand towards her.

Jade reached over and shook his hand. He was tall, maybe a little too thin, with blond hair. He would never be considered handsome, but he had the most compelling cobalt eyes. Normally a male, any male, would ignite the desire. Jade felt nothing sexual for this man at all. That made her uneasy. "Hello, Just Jade," he said, and winked, breaking the spell. "I'm Randy, and this beautiful creature across from you is Helen."

He held her hand longer than was necessary, and was rubbing his thumb across her knuckles.

Jade had the sudden urge to rip her hand out of his grasp, when Helen snapped, "Give the girl back her hand and sit down, Randy."

It was hard not to laugh when Randy dropped her hand like it was on fire, and then nearly missed the chair in his haste to sit down. She covered her mouth, and pretended to cough, hiding the smile she found impossible to stop.

Helen stabbed Jade with her piercing eyes, and winked. "Men," she said and shrugged.

Jade felt the feather light probe in her mind, and quickly reinforced her barriers. She may have had the feeling Randy was reading her mind, but she knew Helen was trying to. She watched the other woman warily, but she simply shrugged. She would have liked a peak into the other woman's mind, but it was against the rules of sanctum, and she was not about to be removed from the one place she knew she would be safe.

For the briefest moment she caught the woman's scent—ginger and oranges. There was nothing threatening there, yet something niggled at the back of her brain before disappearing. Randy played with his food, while covertly peeking at Helen beneath his long lashes, who didn't seem the least aware that he was so smitten with her.

Mrs Gray glared a warning at Helen, who shrugged, her face a mask of innocence. "Help yourself, Miss Jade," Mrs Gray said, keeping her attention on Helen. "We don't like to see our guests to go hungry. Mr Gray always said, 'a full body is a happy body'."

"Thanks, Mrs G. Although you might reconsider your rates when you see how much I can eat."

Helen and Randy exchanged amused looks at the bright shade of pink crawling up the older woman's neck. Mrs Gray muttered something Jade didn't catch, and hurried back to the kitchen.

"How long have you known Charlotte?" Helen asked.

"Charlotte?"

"Mrs Gray."

"I never met her until she opened the door about half an hour ago. Why?"

Helen tipped her head towards the kitchen door. "You seem very familiar with her. I was just wondering how you met. I don't recall seeing you around here before."

Jade helped herself to a large serving of venison and potatoes, poured gravy all over, then added baby carrots to her plate, before replying. "So you're from around here?"

Helen smiled, but it didn't quite reach her eyes. "A long time ago." After several tense moments when no-one spoke, Helen laughed. It was more a nervous laugh than one of humour. "Forget me. So, how long did you say you were staying?"

"I didn't." Jade took a forkful of venison, chewed and swallowed. She wasn't about to broadcast her business to Helen, or anyone else.

They finished their meal in uneasy silence. Jade would have loved some more of that delicious venison, but there was a limit to how much a person could eat in one sitting, and Helen was already paying more attention to Jade than she liked.

Returning to her room, Jade lowered the thermostat on the electric heater and with a wave of her hand lit a fire in the fireplace. She took her time showering and changed into clean jeans and a knit sweater. The temperatures were beginning to rise during the day, but it still got pretty cool at night. She tied her hiking boots, grabbed her vest from the bottom of the bed, and headed out in search of Mrs Gray. She found her in the kitchen doing the dishes.

Jade grabbed a tea towel from the counter and started drying. "Let me help you with these, Mrs G."

Two bright red spots appeared in the woman's cheeks, and she made a grab for the tea towel. Jade pulled it out of her reach. "I can't let you do that, Miss Jade. What would Mr Gray say about me working the guests?"

Jade finished drying the plate and set it on the corner of the table. "You aren't making me do anything I wouldn't do at home." *If Mrs Murphy would let her*. Jade reached for another plate. "Besides, I'm sure Mr Gray, wherever he is, doesn't expect you to do everything yourself."

"Oh my!" The spots on Mrs Gray's cheeks grew. "Mr Gray has been dead these many long years, my dear."

"Do you talk to dead people often?" Jade teased.

"I don't talk to dead people at all!" This time, Mrs Gray caught the towel and tugged it out of Jade's hand. "He talks to me," she mumbled.

She threw the towel on the counter and grabbed the kettle from the stove. "If you must stay in my kitchen, then sit down and let me make you a nice cup of tea."

A wave of homesickness washed over Jade. Mrs Gray reminded her so much of Mrs Murphy. Apparently, neither one would tolerate her in their kitchen. Probably the reason she couldn't cook. "Don't bother yourself, Mrs G." Jade leaned against the edge of the table and watched Mrs Gray flitter around the kitchen. She was really beginning to like the old lady. "I just came down to ask if there were laundry facilities on the premises, or a Laundromat in town."

"It's no bother." Mrs Gray filled the kettle and placed it back on the stove. "Didn't I tell you? The laundry room is in the basement. If you bring your stuff down, I can wash it for you." She took a small tray from beside the fridge and started loading it up with teapot, cups, plates and an apple pie. "I'm making tea for Miss Helen and Randy. They're in the library watching the news on the television. You're welcome to join them."

"If you don't mind, I'd rather sit in here with you?" They could argue about the laundry later. In the meantime maybe Mrs Gray could tell her if any strangers had been around.

The kettle whistled and Mrs Gray added water to the teapot. "Just let me take this to the others and I'll make us a cup."

It was peaceful sitting in the kitchen, with the warmth of the woodstove and the fresh scent of the pines drifting through the open window. When Mrs Gray returned she added two scoops from a fancy jar on the counter, and boiling water to another teapot. Then she opened the fridge and started pulling out more food. Next she began cutting huge slices off a loaf of fresh bread.

"I was going to make myself a nice venison sandwich," she said, as she cut several slices. "Would you care for one?"

Jade began to salivate. It had been what, a whole twenty minutes since she had eaten? "I'd love one."

The outside door suddenly swung in. There had been no knock. From where Jade was sitting she couldn't see who entered, but from the wide smile on Mrs Gray's face they were definitely welcome.

"Luke, you're back. We weren't expecting you until tomorrow. I was just making some venison sandwiches. Sit down and I'll bring you yours."

As the door began to swing shut the man spoke. "Reading my mind again, Charlotte?"

Goosebumps traveled along Jade's skin and her heart fluttered, as the deep rumbling voice caressed her. It wasn't possible. The door closed and Jade found herself staring into the pale brown eyes of last night's stranger.

"You!" They cried in unison.

Chapter Seventeen

Luke snapped off the radio with a snarl. What the hell was going on? In over a hundred years no *wolf* has dared attack a human in his territory. And now this. If news got out there would be wide spread panic and every wolf, dog, and Lycan would be in danger. When humans were afraid they were more terrifying than the *Moarté.*

Luke grabbed his cell phone and flipped it open. The no service message slid across the screen. "Useless piece of junk." He jammed the phone back into its charger and sighed. There was no sense in trying the phone until he made it through the rock cut.

Luke had felt the magic in the park, and to be honest it had him worried. It was not the usual magic associated with a *were*. The magic he had felt was strong. Powerful. It had been cloaking the park, and Luke had been unable to pinpoint its location.

He was forced to give up his search for the mystery woman, even while every nerve in his body screamed he continue. *He had never met anyone like her before. She was powerful. There was no doubt about it. But what was she? Not lycan. He would know if she was lycan. Who and what was she? The most important thing would he see her again?*

Luke couldn't worry about any of that now. He had to get back to Willow Bend and tell Daniel and Grégoire what had happened. The Matei twins were not only the law in Willow Bend; they were also his right and left arms. He had no doubt that together they would be able to track the rogue.

Who are you? The fact that he couldn't seem to keep his thoughts from her was a little disconcerting. He hadn't felt like this about a woman since Tasha -- *and look where that had gotten them.*

For centuries their pack had been the protectors of the ruling family of Transylvania. Until Luke met Natasha. He had fallen for her like a fly zapped with Raid. Hard and fast. He wanted to spend his life with her, and had foolishly told his secret without waiting for the approval of the pack. The morning of their planned wedding she had betrayed them all. The villagers had attacked and massacred nearly their entire pack, forcing the handful of survivors, mostly children, to flee to safety. They had eventually made their way across an ocean to forge a new life for them in this remote wilderness. Luke once again pushed the unsettling thoughts to the back of his mind, and tried to concentrate on the present.

Luke tried the phone again, this time able to put his call through.

"Hey, Boss. What's up?"

He might have been gone for almost three months, but Daniel had known the second Luke had come within three hundred miles of home.

"There's been a killing."

Luke could tell by the silence on the other end that Daniel was as stunned as he had been. He filled them in with the little he knew. The minute he arrived at the police station, the three of them began searching for any sign of a stranger. This was something they had to deal with, the sooner the better.

Willow Bend was a small, closely-knit community. If a stranger came to town, someone, somewhere, would know about it.

Nothing.

Luke should have been relieved, but he wasn't. He *knew* the wolf had come here. With thousands of acres of forest and mountain there were thousands of places for a wolf to hide.

Luke was in the twins' office when the call came in about Michael Green. His wife, Debbie, was hysterical but they knew it was bad. Michael had been renting a house about ten miles from town ever since he and his wife had split up.

The hackles on the back of Luke's neck rose the moment he entered the house, and the familiar tingle of spent magic, and something more, surrounded him. It reminded him of the park.

Luke looked at Grégoire. "Do you feel it?"

"Yeah, Boss. I'm sure I can feel *Moarté*, but I wouldn't want to bet the farm on it." Grégoire looked anything but pleased with the possibility. The *Moarté* or "Death Squad" didn't leave trace scents but they did sometimes leave traces of their magic.

Daniel stayed outside with Debbie until the paramedics came and gave her something to calm her down, then he told them to take her to the hospital. "You can't do anything for Michael, but you can take care of his wife. He would have wanted that."

He squeezed Debbie's hand and helped her into the back of the ambulance. Debbie and his wife, Sondra, were co-owners of the Haberdashery in town. Deb and Michael had been guests in their house on a regular basis. "It'll be okay, Deb. We'll find whoever is responsible for this."

Daniel slammed the door on the ambulance. "Do me a favour, Mike? Give Steven a call and tell him to bring the wagon. Warn him it's messy."

"Sure thing, Chief." Daniel was technically just a deputy, but he didn't bother correcting him. Most people couldn't tell the difference between his brother and him.

Entering the house, Daniel wrinkled his nose in disgust. "What kind of animal would do this?"

Grégoire shrugged. "Use your nose, baby brother, and tell us." The older by three minutes, Grégoire never passed up an opportunity to rib Daniel. A fact Daniel took in stride, along with the crack about his olfactory powers. They both knew Grégoire's sense of smell was four times that of his brother, who couldn't smell his way out of a brown paper sack. However, what Daniel lacked in the sense of smell, he made up for with his advanced psychic abilities.

"I don't know, Bro. There's so much residual violence."

After a thorough search of the house they knew that a man had entered, and a wolf had left. A confused, scared, and very dangerous wolf. Unfortunately for them, he hadn't left any tracks they could follow, and its scent had already dissipated. And it looked like the *Moarté* was already in town.

An hour later, Luke opened the door of his private quarters to a persistent ringing. He dropped his suitcase in the middle of the hall and grabbed the phone. "Yeah?"

"You're wanted at the Sanctum." Click. Elizabeth hated using the phone even more than Luke.

Leaving the car Luke shifted and ran the short distance to The Inner Sanctum. Shifting back to man, he had just lifted the knocker when the door swung in on silent hinges, allowing him a view of Charlotte's familiar round face. Bless her soul. With Charlotte around you didn't need knockers.

"Luke, you're back. We weren't expecting you until tomorrow. I was just making venison sandwiches. Sit down and I'll bring you yours."

"Reading my mind, again Charlotte?" Luke took two steps into the room, picked Charlotte up in a big bear hug, kissed her soundly on both cheeks, and then set her back on her feet. The door swung shut and Luke blinked, not quite believing what his eyes were seeing. Sitting at Charlotte's table, and looking even more beautiful in her casual pants and form hugging knit-sweater, was his mystery woman.

"You!" They blurted simultaneously.

Umpteen questions flashed through Luke's mind. What was she doing here? Had she followed him? Did she have anything to do with what was going on? Who was she? How had she found him? Most importantly ... *How was he going to keep her here?*

His arms ached to wrap themselves around her. His lips burned for her kisses. She was a candle and he the lowly moth attracted to her smouldering flame. He took a step towards her, unable to stop himself.

Surprise, swiftly followed by wariness, and something else flickered in her wide amber eyes. The musky scent of her desire rolled off her in waves, circling and caressing him. He became instantly hard.

Luke stopped his approach, struggling to bring himself under control. He was standing there awkwardly trying to will away his hard-on, when the door to the hall opened and Helen strolled in. Spying Luke, she ran across the kitchen and threw herself at him. He staggered, and wrapped his arms around her to keep them both from falling. Her arms circled his neck, and she planted a huge, noisy kiss on his cheek.

Happy to see her, Luke swung his sister around before setting her back on her feet. "When did you get here?" Luke asked.

"If you will excuse me I'll leave you two alone." Her voice was low and husky, and pain flickered across her amber eyes. In one fluid motion she rose from her seat, grabbed the vest from the back of her chair, and headed for the door. "I'm sorry, Mrs. Gray, but I'll have to pass on that sandwich. I just remembered someplace I have to be."

Luke stared at the closed door in stunned silence. What the hell had just happened? He'd had her in his grasp and just as suddenly she was gone. He took two steps towards the door before realizing Helen was tugging on his arm. "What?" He almost growled the word.

Helen put her hands on her hips and her brows narrowed as she glared back at him. "What's with you and Jade anyway?" she demanded. "I haven't seen you in over two years and you don't even notice me."

Luke grabbed his sister by the shoulders, ignoring her startled gasp. "What did you call her?"

Helen shook his hands off and continued to glare at him. "Don't bully me, Big Brother. If you want to know something, ask."

Luke took a deep, calming breath, shoved his fingers through his unruly locks, and smiled at his sister, although it didn't quite reach his eyes. "You're right, Sis. I'm sorry, and I'm asking."

Charlotte set a plate on the table, and the tantalizing aroma of venison reached his nostrils. Luke's stomach rumbled with hunger and he was torn between the meal in front of him and the woman who had just left the sanctum. Hunger won. Besides, deep down he knew the woman would be back, and he had to find out why Helen was in town.

He chose the chair Jade just vacated. It was still warm, and her scent lingered. He inhaled the sweet fragrance, allowing it to comfort him with the knowledge she was near, and turned to his sister. "Sit with me while I eat and we can talk."

Luke took two bites and devoured half the sandwich. Licking his lips he grinned at Charlotte. "Delicious as ever, Charlie."

Charlotte turned bright pink and busied herself at the sink. "If you need another let me know. No sense wasting a good roast."

Luke finished his first sandwich before turning to his sister. He wanted to bombard her with questions about Jade, but decided against it. He didn't want his sister speculating about his interest. Instead, he took a bite of his second sandwich, chewed more slowly this time, then swallowed and asked. "What are you doing here? Thomas told me you were in Paris shopping."

Anger flashed in Helen's midnight eyes. "That Bitch wouldn't let me in to see Gemma."

By bitch, she meant Elizabeth. Fifty years ago, Helen had challenged the pack's alpha female, and lost. According to Lycan law Helen's life was forfeit, but because she was Luke's sister, Elizabeth had chosen to banish her instead. Thomas Radu had declared his love for Helen on that day, and he had asked permission to leave with Helen. Unwilling to lose one of his best friends, and his only living blood relative, Luke had sent them to Italy where they had begun a new pack. According to Lycan law, once banished Helen could never return to Willow Creek. If she did, the death penalty could be invoked.

Yet here she was.

Luke counted to ten, silently. "What are you doing here, Helen? You know our laws."

Helen's dark eyes flashed. "What do I care for laws when my baby needs me?"

Luke shook his head in frustration, when what he really wanted to do was strangle his sister. When it came to Gemma, Helen was the doting, overprotective mother. The moon rose and set on that girl, and Helen had spoiled her to no end. Luke was amazed Gemma wasn't an obnoxious brat, considering the way her mother treated her. "Gemma is a big girl, Helen. She has chosen to come here to study. Both you and Thomas agreed that this was the best place for her right now. You can't keep her your baby forever."

Helen rolled her eyes. "I know all that. I came because something is wrong." She hurried on before Luke could interrupt. She may not be psychic, but she did have a very strong bond with her child. "Two weeks ago I woke up knowing something had happened to Gemma. I could taste her fear. I felt her pain. My heart nearly stopped. I caught the first plane here, and went straight to 'The Den', but *She* wouldn't let me in. She refused to even tell Gemma, my own daughter, that I was here. And she continually intercepts my phone calls."

Helen reached out and placed her hand over her brother's. "You have to find out what's wrong and fix it, Luke. You're responsible for the welfare of the pack. As much as I hate to admit it, as long as Gemma is here she is part of your pack. Protect my baby."

Luke placed his free hand over his sister's, and squeezed. "I swear on Gheorgès grave that I will protect Gemma with my life. I also need to keep you safe. You need to go back to Italy. Back to Thomas. And don't come here again." Luke gave his sister a crooked grin. "They make phones for occasions like this. Use them."

Luke stood, leaned over and gave his sister a kiss on the cheek. "I'll send a driver to take you to the airport."

Chapter Eighteen

Gemma locked the front door, and flipped the sign to `closed`. Not that anyone would show up tonight expecting the Center to be open. They ran one overnight camping trip on the first night of the full moon over at Wolf Lake Falls, and closed the center for the next two days. It had been that way since the beginning.

This time was for the wolves. They were already gathering. Gemma could feel them all around her. They would stay out of sight until all of the uninitiated humans had left for their homes. Then they would hunt undisturbed in their territory, and afterward the unattached wolves would pair up and have sex. Hot, unadulterated, no strings attached sex. You couldn't call it anything else without feelings involved, except for instant sexual gratification. It was the same in all the packs.

Gemma had never been allowed to stay after the hunt. Her mother protected her with a fierceness that kept even the bravest wolf away. She still treated Gemma like a child, although she was almost twenty years old. She was almost suffocating at times, and her father was just as bad. Even if she had dared to disobey her parents and stay after the hunt, nobody in her pack would tempt the wrath of her parents and choose her.

Not everyone stayed after the hunt. Those with mates usually went their separate ways.

Many of the wolves capable of staying in human form, chose to party at Wulfson Mansion. Many single wolves lived at the mansion. Already virile they were nearly impossible to deny during their peak. Luke Wulfson had turned the old mansion, built at the turn of the eighteenth century in the fashion of the antebellum estates in New Orleans, into a shared home for the Lycan community. Once a month, in deference to the pull of the moon, Luke hosted the Moon Phase Dance. That way he could control, somewhat, the appetites of his wolves, making sure they didn't lose complete control.

Rules for admittance were strict, ensuring the safety of both human and wolf. Lycan children spent the night at the Hub with adult supervision. Sara and Gemma often volunteered to help with the young ones.

"Earth to Gemma. Earth to Gemma." Sara snapped her fingers in front of Gemma's face.

Gemma blinked. "I'm sorry, Sara. What did you say?"

"I asked if you were coming to the Hub tonight." With attendance restricted to twenty-five and older, Sara was too young for the dances, and if Gemma's parents had their way she would never be allowed to attend. Hell, if her parents found out she'd gone to the bar with Sara she'd be sent back to Italy ... yesterday.

Gemma reached into the pocket of her spring jacket, and fingered the cold metal of handcuffs laying there. If Daniel found out that his son Greg had lent them to her, they would both be in a world of trouble. "I don't think so, Sara. There's something I have to do tonight."

"What's up with you, Gem? Are you okay? You've been distracted all day."

Gemma eyed her friend warily. "What do you mean?"

"Well. For one thing, you haven't even asked how it went with George last night."

Gemma noticed the concerned on her friend's face, and forced herself to smile. "Well. For one thing," she repeated her friend's words. "We worked in different departments all day. I haven't seen you for more than five minutes at a time."

"Yeah, and you were distracted the whole five minutes."

Gemma locked elbows with her friend and led her towards the parking lot. "Okay, Sara, out with it. I can tell you are dying to tell me what happened."

"Forget that. I want to know what's going on with you."

Gemma shrugged. She couldn't very well tell her best friend that she thought she turned into a wolf and killed someone last night. "I just haven't been sleeping very well lately," she said instead. She glanced up towards the rising moon and hurried her step towards the parking lot. "Do tell. What happened last night?"

Sara rolled her eyes and let out an exaggerated sigh. "Nothing. George was being his usual obnoxious self." Then she giggled. "'Til midnight."

It was Gemma's turn to roll her eyes. Her friend would stretch this out all night if she let her. "What happened at midnight?"

"He kissed me."

"He what?" George kissed Sara. What was the world coming to? Those two could barely stand each other. If George hurt her best friend, Gemma would kill him.

Sara dimpled. Gemma was astounded to see Sara actually blush. She hadn't known Sara could blush.

"He kissed me. And I liked it." Sara tugged on Gemma's arm. "I liked it, Gem. What am I supposed to do now?"

Gemma laughed. Almost. For as long as she'd known her, Sara had never been at a loss as to what to do with a boy. "What do you want to do?" She asked warily. She should warn Sara to turn tail and run. She knew the effect George had on women during the moon phase. The pheromones alone would have her doing flips in his bed. Although Sara was usually more than a match for any man, she had no idea the trouble she could get into with a wolf. Gemma should warn her friend, but how? She couldn't very well tell Sara that George was the epitome of the big bad wolf.

"You girls talking about me?" They both jumped at the deep, rumbling voice.

"George! What's wrong with you? Sneaking up on us like that." Sara glared at George. "And we were not talking about you." Gemma flinched when Sara pinched her arm, but she didn't dare contradict her friend.

"As a matter of fact," Sara continued, her voice breezy. "I was just asking Gemma if she was coming to the Hub with Mark and me tonight."

"Mark." George growled the name "is not welcome at the Hub."

Sara removed her arm from Gemma's, and shrugged. "In that case, I guess I won't be going to the Hub after all." She winked at Gemma, then got in her car, started the engine and drove away spraying gravel at George.

Gemma had never seen George's face turn quite that shade of red. It was almost purple. She could practically see steam coming out his ears. It was a struggle not to laugh.

"One of these days I am going to give that girl exactly what she deserves."

Gemma burst out laughing. It was the first time all week, and it actually felt good. George glared at her, and she laughed even harder. Then wiping the tears from her eyes, she patted him on the arm, and teased. "It's good to see some things never change."

George laughed too. He put his arm around Gemma's shoulder and gave her a squeeze. "So? How about you? Going to the Hub tonight?"

Gemma thought about the handcuffs in her pocket, and shook her head. "Sorry, George. I have previous plans."

"Are you joining the hunt?" The shock in his voice, almost made her cringe.

Would nobody consider her an adult? "Not tonight. I have something I need to do at home."

"In that case, can you drop me off at the Hub on the way by? I was hoping to catch a ride with Sara, but it doesn't look like that's going to happening."

"You're not hunting tonight?"

George's grin was devilish. "Yeah. Later. I'm meeting Tony and we're heading over to the Strawberry-Moon Dance."

That so wasn't fair. Tony was still a child in more ways that Gemma, but nobody would refuse him admittance to the dance just because he was male. Gemma waved at George, blew a kiss at Tony who was waiting outside the Hub, and drove home. It didn't matter what she thought. Pack law was Pack law and she wasn't about to change it.

At the cabin, she heated up some tomato soup, which she ate with a ham and cheese sandwich. By the time the first moonbeam shone through her living room window, she had locked the doors and undressed. She might have been able to shift since she was eleven, but Gemma still couldn't control the magic enough not to destroy her clothes when she shifted. When the clock struck eight, she was handcuffed to the steel frame of her bed.

This wolf would not be running free tonight.

Chapter Nineteen

Stupid. Stupid. Stupid. How could she be so stupid?

A married man? Jade could just die from the shame of it. Not that it was all her fault. He had been just as eager as she had been. Maybe even more so.

No. She wasn't going to pass the blame onto him just because he was a man. She was the one who had gone out specifically to satisfy her own needs. He couldn't help himself. She knew the power pheromones had on the opposite sex. She had been the victim of them more than once herself over the years.

No, it wasn't his fault. She had chosen him the moment she had laid eyes on him.

Still the pain had been unbelievable when Helen ran across the room and threw her arms around him. Jade had wanted to claw her eyes out. She couldn't believe the effect this man had on her. It was really stupid, considering she didn't know his name, and he was married. For the first time since her disastrous marriage, she had found herself wanting more from a man than just sex.

The first time she had felt the magic of the moon on her hormones, she thought she was in love. Unfortunately for them both, the boy she chose thought so too. They were both young and naïve, and had allowed their raging hormones to lead them straight to the altar. She tried to make it work, but after three years of fighting, except during the full moon at which times they never left the bedroom, they divorced. She should have known better. Marriage wasn't in the cards for her. Not then … Not now.

Jade wondered if her mother had felt that way before she'd met Jade's father. Jade's father was a very special man. Irish, born and raised, he'd left his homeland in his teens and moved to the States, where he became a police officer.

He met Jade's mother while on a case, and it was love at first sight. It was during the full moon, but Jade's mother was older and more mature than Jade had been, and she had learned not to let herself get carried away by the pull of the moon. Her father liked to tell Jade it only took two months of chasing her, before Caer finally turned around and caught him. Three months after they'd first laid eyes on each other they were wed. Cerridwen blessed their marriage and nine months later Jade was born. Jade still dreamed of one day meeting a man like her father.

Leaning against the closed door, Jade let her hand stray to her short locks. She could never compete with a woman like Helen.

Helen was so much like Jade's mother. Both were beautiful beyond measure and wore their hair in a long plait down their backs. As a child Jade had loved her mother's hair, and had insisted her mother plait hers in the exact same way. Then, at age five, Jade's ideal world had come crashing down around her small shoulders. A group of vampires had banded together to destroy her mother. Jade had watched from her hiding spot in the closet as monster after monster had exploded. She was not afraid because she had seen her mother fight before and her mother always won.

Soon there was only one left. Her little heart almost stopped when the monster wrapped her mother's beautiful long braid around his hand. Her mother's head was pulled back, and her slender white throat was exposed. The pulse on the side of her neck beat in time with Jade's own heart. Jade watched in frozen helplessness as the vampire reached in front of her mother with his free hand. His middle fingernail grew a lethal three inches. Slowly he slid it from one side of her mother's throat to the other. Caer's eyes widen with the realization she was dying. She stopped struggling, and threw her arm behind her, thrusting it into the vampire's chest. She brought it back with the vampire's black heart still beating in her palm. His body slowly disintegrated and when he was gone, Caer's severed head fell to the floor. Her body followed with a soft thud.

Jade had cut her own plait off the next morning, and vowed she would never let it grow again. When it came to sexy or safe, she would choose safe every time.

Still shaking from the horror of her memories, Jade pushed herself away from the door. She didn't have time for daydreams or memories. There was a killer out there and her job was to stop him. She put her vest on, leaned down to retie her hiking boot, *she really did need to get new laces,* then took two steps into the woods before shifting into an owl.

On silent wings she lifted herself into the sky, familiarizing herself with the geography. It was so peaceful up here, away from the world and all its problems. Higher and higher she soared, as the world got smaller and smaller, until it was nothing but a road map. Jade had no problem making out the rivers, lakes, and roads crisscrossing the countryside. She called on the memory of the map at the information center to identify her surroundings. Stormy Lake, where the Inner Sanctum was situated, the next lake over was originally *Tamiita-de-cimp,* which was Romanian for ground pine, but in recent years had been officially changed to Pine Lake. The main road completely circled Stormy Lake, with different spars leading into the forest and towards the mountains. The road didn't go completely around

Pine Lake. Instead it ended on the north side at the entrance to a large estate, while joining the highway on the south side. A few houses dotted the lakeshore with most of it being unpopulated.

The owl drifted silently downward until it could make out the different birch, pine and maple trees.

It followed a branch in the main road that ran from the highway across the bridge between Sycamore and Stormy Lakes, straight to the Wolf Center about five kilometres away. There were already several wolves beginning to gather there. They didn't appear threatening and Jade ignored them. Instead she flew across the lake to the west end of town. This was where she lost the trail earlier so it was as good a place as any to start the search again.

On this side of the lakes, the highway doubled as Main Street. Most of the shops were already closed for the evening, with two restaurants and one bar in town still open. In human form, Jade wandered between the buildings, searching the dumpsters and out buildings behind them. Satisfied that nobody, or nothing, was hiding there, she entered the first restaurant.

Ordering a burger and cola she found a chair in the back corner where she could see everything going on in the room; which wasn't much. Other than herself, there were two women, one man, who surprisingly didn't interest her in the least, and a couple of teenagers. All were human. She listened to the idle conversation for a while, but nobody mentioned a stranger. Surprisingly nobody mentioned the murder, which meant that the cops were keeping it quiet for now.

Wiping her mouth, Jade left a tip under her plate and walked to the next restaurant. The burgers here were much better, but the occupants all human, were of no more help than the others. Jade finished her burger and headed for the Waterfront Bar.

Jade entered to the sounds of "Boot Scootin' Boogie" blaring from the jukebox. Ignoring the mostly empty tables scattered around, Jade crossed the dance floor easily avoided the few dancers there. Most of the crowd was in their late forties, early fifties, and the conversations ran the gamut from grandchildren to fishing. Jade returned the smiles and nods of a few, while ignoring the suspicious glares from others. She was used to small town mentalities. Unless you were born and raised in a place, you were considered a stranger--which should make it easy to find one.

Ordering a beer, she listened as Billy Ray Cyrus began to belt out "Achy Breaky Heart", and took a stool at the bar. Within seconds a tall, darkly handsome man pulled the stool beside hers closer, and sat down.

"New in town?" He moved his stool even closer so his leg pressed against hers. He leaned his elbow on the bar and flashed a smile she knew was meant to melt her heart, or at least her inhibitions. It did absolutely nothing for her.

Jade ignored the pressure of his leg. "What makes you think so?" She sipped her beer while studying him over the bottle. His smile was pleasant enough, but there was no mistaking the leer in his blue eyes, even in this dim light.

"I haven't seen you around before."

"What do you want, Dave?" The bartender wiped the counter, purposely knocking Dave's arm out from under him.

Dave glared at the bartender, who was a cute twenty something. "Why do care, Sue? You dumped me. Remember?"

Great! This was exactly where she wanted to be; the middle of a lover's quarrel. Was she destined to be the other woman?

"Get over yourself, Dave. I don't care what you do or who you do it with." It sure sounded to Jade like she cared. "Do you want a beer or not?"

Telltale scarlet began to creep up his neck and his voice became harsh. "Of course I want a beer. Why else would I be here?"

"Why else indeed?"

Sue returned and slammed a bottle of beer on the counter. Dave grabbed it, then turned and reached for Jade's arm. "Let's sit over there," he said, pointing to a table away from the bar.

Jade saw the hurt in the girl's eyes. "I'm quite comfortable here," she said. "I can't stay long anyway. I was just looking for a friend of mine. Have you seen any other strangers in town lately? He should have arrived earlier tonight. I'm not sure where he's staying though."

"Sorry, haven't seen anyone. If I were new in town, I'd want to stay at the Inner Sanctum. It's a real cool castle across the lake."

Unless Randy had her completely fooled, he wasn't there.

A wolf howled somewhere nearby. "Was that a wolf?"

"Sure was."

Jade turned in her chair so she could see out over the lake. The moon sparkled on the water, lighting a path almost to the other side. "Are there very many wolves around here?"

Dave shifted uncomfortably on his stool, and seemed to find his beer bottle suddenly fascinating. "There are a few," he mumbled.

Jade could sense Dave's reluctance to talk about the wolves, but she pressed on anyway. "Are they dangerous?" She leaned towards him and whispered, just the right amount of nervousness present in her voice.

"They're all dangerous as far as I'm concerned," he mumbled. "And stranger."

"What do you mean?" Jade sat back, and watched Dave over the top of her beer as she took another sip.

He glanced at the other occupants of the room, and then watched Sue pour a drink. Finally he stared at an invisible spot on the countertop. "Nothing." He finished his beer and called to Sue to bring him another.

Jade declined his offer of another beer and changed the subject. "Where's the hot spot in town?"

Dave ogled her lewdly, and raised his eyebrows in an attempt to look debonair. "My place." He said all the right things, but he couldn't keep his eyes off Sue at the other end of the bar.

Jade ignored his comment, and watched him watch Sue, like a tiger ready to pounce. It would be obvious to a blind man that his interest lay at the other end of the bar.

Jade relaxed and found her mind wondering to last night. She reminded herself he was married, put his memory away, and turned her attention back to Dave. "So why did your girlfriend break up with you?"

"It's stupid really." He took a gulp of beer, his eyes never leaving Sue as she served drinks to the other customers. "We had a big fight about the dance over at the mansion."

Jade's interest perked. "Dance?" He had to mean Wulfson Mansion. If there was a dance there tonight, she might be able to sneak in and get a peek at the leader of the pack before her meeting with him in a couple of days. "That's at the end of Tamiita-de-cimp, isn't it?"

"Yeah. But nobody calls it that anymore. That place is cool. Built like that mansion in the movie 'Gone With the Wind'. You know the one I mean. My mom has that movie on VCR and must have made us kids watch it at least a dozen times. She was always pointing out the similarities between that mansion and Wulfson Mansion. Myself, I prefer The Inner Sanctum. Now there's a real castle. Has a dungeon and everything. I took Sue there last Halloween."

Jade tried to get Dave back on the subject that interested her most. "Tell me about this dance."

"Once a month, always during the full moon, they have a Moon-Phase Dance. This month it's the Strawberry Moon."

"Is that what they call it these days? Dancing?" They both jumped as an old man slammed his empty bottle on the counter between them. "No decent citizen would be caught dead at one of those so called dances. Never let my sons go." He glared at Dave. "... I won't let my grandchild go either. Those dances should be banned."

Sue came over and picked up the empty bottle. "Goodnight, Gramps," she said. "Don't forget to tell Grams thanks for the pie."

The old man's face broke out into a wide smile, and his blue eyes twinkled. "I sure won't, Sue. And don't you forget what I said about those dances." He glared once more at Dave and left the bar.

"That," Dave watched the old man leave the bar, "Is why Sue broke up with me. Her grandfather overheard me and a friend talking about the dance. He told Sue and she assumed I wanted to go."

"Do you? Want to go, I mean."

"Hell no. That's the thing. I've never been. I've never wanted to go. I love Sue, but her grandfather has her convinced I would rather be there than with her."

"Why don't you try telling Sue the truth?"

Dave drained the last of his beer. "She won't believe me."

"It doesn't hurt to try." Jade saw the way Sue looked at Dave, whenever he wasn't looking at her. She was pretty sure Sue wanted to believe Dave. She just needed a little encouragement.

Jade finished her own beer and said her goodbyes. She would make another patrol around town, before expanding her search further.

Chapter Twenty

The moon stirred her passion. The wind whispered to her.

The owl perched on the branch of a birch, wide amber eyes taking in the activity below. Just a few candles illuminated the stone walkway from the gates to the main entrance of the house. The candles were probably more to set the mood than anything else. The sky was free from clouds, and between the stars and the brilliance of the moon, no artificial light was required.

"Sorry, sweetheart. I can't let you in tonight."

The guard, tall, dark and delicious enough to eat, was talking to a woman in her thirties who could barely stand up. Even from where she perched, Jade could tell the woman was more than a little inebriated.

"What?" Her shrill voice jarred on the ears.

"You know the rules. No drinking."

The owl listened to their conversation, pleased to learn there were at least some rules to the mating rituals.

"Oh, please," the girl continued, stretching out the please. "You know me. I've been here at least a dozen times. We've even danced together." She added the latter with, what she probably believed was a seductive wink, but looked more like someone trying to keep both eyes open.

She teetered vicariously on her high heels. The guard reached out to steady her before she landed on her face. The woman, who appeared to be in her thirties, brushed the guards hands away, and reached for the gate. In a fluid motion, the guard reclaimed her arm, turned her back towards him, and pulled a cell phone from his pocket.

"Sorry, sweetheart, but rules are rules. They're there to protect you as well as us." He pushed the recall button on his phone, and waited for someone to answer. "I'll have a cab take you home."

"I don't want to go home." The woman pouted prettily, realized she was getting nowhere, and let her body relax against the guards. "Why don't you take me home?"

"Not tonight, darling," he drawled. His voice was enough to make any woman's toes curl.

He spoke quietly into the phone and within minutes a cab pulled up. The guard helped settle the woman in the back seat, before handing several bills to the driver. "Make sure she gets home safe," he said. "Don't drop her off anywhere else."

The cab left only to be replaced by another. This one was carrying several women, all wearing low cut, and body hugging outfits, or short flowing dresses which barely concealed them.

The owl left its perch and flew to a spot just out of sight of the gates. In the blink of an eye Jade was standing in the center of the road. She had chosen a low cut, halter style dress with a short, flimsy, flyaway skirt in blood red. Not bad. She glanced down at her bare feet and frowned. One would think that after fifty years she could get the shoes right.

Jade closed her eyes and concentrated. When she opened them again, she was wearing a pair of black leather sandals with two-inch heels. Much better. She walked around the bend and approached the gate. The low, appreciative whistle coming from the bushes beside the gate sent a shiver down her spine. She turned towards the sound to watch the same guard emerge. He was even better looking up close.

He took his time as his eyes traveled from the top of her head to the tips of her bare toes. The feminine part of her thrilled at the hungry look in his eyes, but to her amazement, other than a deep appreciation of his masculine beauty, Jade felt nothing at all.

"You're new." Curiosity warred with the hunger in his eyes.

"I'm staying over at the Inner Sanctum for a few days." Would she even be granted access to the house? For all she knew, these dances could be by invitation only. If that were the case, in all probability, she wasn't going to find the killer here. Even if it wasn't the case, she didn't really think she was going to find him here. She had searched the town and the surrounding woods for any sign of a disturbance, but had found nothing. Either her prey was in human form, sleeping, or he had learned to control his hunger.

For several hours she had been trying to ignore the lure of this place, but every breeze carried it to her. The hunger inside that building called to the hunger in her until she thought she would go insane. Finally she admitted, at least to herself, that if she was going to function enough to do her job, first she would have to get a fix for her craving.

A crackling came from the guard's walkie-talkie and they both jumped. The guard pulled it from the clip on his belt and a statically metallic voice said, "What's the hold-up down there. You trying to keep the pretty lady for yourself, Mike?"

Mike glared somewhere to the right of the gate, held the button on his walkie-talkie and snarled. "Maybe. And maybe I'm just waiting for you to get your sorry ass back down here so I can escort the pretty lady to the house myself."

Jade kept one ear on the conversation, while checking out the area surrounding the gate. For the first time she noticed the camera mounted halfway up a tree near the gate and almost hidden from view by the leaves.

"No can do, buddy," the disembodied voice crackled.

Jade tuned in to the life all around her. Crickets chirped merrily, accompanied every so often by the soft, almost scratchy hoot of a barn owl. Several bats swooped over the open water dining on insects, while raccoons fished in the shallow waters for a meal of clams. A loon called to its mate somewhere in the distance. Several wolves were wandering in the gardens past the gate, and music drifted from the mansion.

The music called to something deep inside. A hunger. A need to be wild and free. It teased the animal side of her, begging for its release. Jade's foot began to tap to the beat of CCR's "Bad Moon Rising."

"Miss?"

Jade spun towards the guard. When had he quit talking on the radio? "I'm sorry. Did you say something?"

Mike held the gate open. "If you stay on the path it'll bring you to the front doors of the house.

Jade smiled her thanks, and stepped through the open gate. She heard him groan behind her, and ignored his muttered "I'm going to kill you for this, Tony." Jade followed the flagstone path, the candles more than enough to light the way, and the wolves keeping to the shadows.

"Don't worry about the wolves." Mike's voice drifted to her on the breeze. "They won't bother you." His nearly inaudible "unless you want them to," had Jade smiling to herself.

Jade was beginning to feel like Little Red Riding Hood on her way to grandma's house with the big bad wolf lurking behind every tree, just waiting to pounce. Trepidation kept her moving slow, that and walking on heels. She should be out looking for the killer. Instead she let her hormones lead her to the one place she was guaranteed he wouldn't be. She should turn around, now, before it was too late.

She kept on walking.

The door opened as Jade approached, and several drop-dead gorgeous men surrounded her and propelled her inside. Nobody actually touched her, but their hunger was so intense it felt like they were all over her. The youngest among them leaned towards her, and inhaled deeply.

"Are you sniffing me?" she asked the obvious. She didn't have to sniff anyone. Lust rolled off them in waves. The female part of her thrilled to their attention, and yet not one of these men appealed to her.

The young man jumped back, his neck and ears crimson. "No ... no," he stammered, and began to cough.

Several of the others laughed, while the one closest to him patted him on the back. "Don't mind him," he said. "This is his first dance."

Jade turned her eyes demurely to the floor, and allowed a slight smile to come to her lips. "Mine too," she said in a quiet voice.

The foyer was the size of three average living rooms, with diamond chandeliers and floors polished to a reflective shine. Music came from a live band set up on a stage at the far end. The band itself consisted of five of the hottest men. Thoughts of sex ran rampant through her mind, and yet she couldn't picture herself with any of these men. She couldn't say the same for the other women. They were practically drooling, and not just for the band. Every man in the room reeked of lust.

Jade recognized the song the band was singing as Franz Ferdinand's "Do you want to" and by the look of the dancers on the floor, and the people milling around off the dance floor, more than one person was getting lucky tonight.

Someone grabbed her hand, and dragged Jade to the dance floor. The music was a living entity that took control, and Jade moved to the beat.

"You're new around here." It was a statement.

There was something comforting about her partner. It might have been the fact that he wasn't looking at her like he was about to pounce and devour her. She found herself wanting to tell him everything. "I just got here today."

Another male sidled up to her and leaned his body into hers, whispering in her ear. "Why don't you ditch the old man and try me?" His voice was a study in smooth seduction sending shivers across her skin.

The old man, as the youth referred to him could have passed for late thirties, early forties. He held her closer, and practically growled at the youth. "Back off Tony."

Tony put both hands in the air and stepped back in surrender. "Hey, I was just trying to show the girl a good time. Not to mention trying to save your ass, old man. I wouldn't want to be in your place when Sondra finds out you were dancing with this pretty young thing."

Jade stopped dancing and stared at the two men. Great. Just what she needed tonight, another married man.

Tony smiled at the older man in triumph, only to have his smile dashed when the older man shrugged. "Since when does my sister-in-law care who I dance with?"

The music changed to "Little Red Riding Hood" which Jade found rather fitting, as she was pulled into another dance.

The outer door opened and a hush fell over the room. Jade didn't have to turn around to know who had arrived. Every nerve in her body hummed like a finely tuned violin. She was aware the instant he stood behind her, and wasn't a bit surprised that her dance partner had faded into the crowd.

"You *better* watch out." His voice was a long awaited lover's caress, a drop of cool water for a parched soul, the sun after a week's rain.

All thoughts of Helen disappeared like fine mist. "Why's that?" Her voice was an unbecoming squeak.

He grinned wickedly, and Jade felt her toes curl. "You're in my woods now."

He moved closer and Jade backed away. The music and the crowd faded until they were the only two in the room.

Jade felt the wall solid against her back, and stopped. Luke kept moving until he was pressing against her and she couldn't help notice the evidence of his interest. Her bones melted and her stomach muscles clenched. Slowly, ever so slowly, his head tipped towards hers. Jade had plenty of time to move, to avoid the connection; her lips parted slightly in anticipation of the kiss. Her breath came in short, quick spurts.

An image of ebony tresses and coal-black eyes popped unbidden into her head. Jade's blood froze in her veins and she averted her head. "What about Helen?" she whispered.

"Helen?" The stunned look on Luke's face was almost comical. "What does my sister have to do with anything?"

"Your sister!" Relief bubbled to the surface and Jade began to laugh. Several faces turned their way but Jade ignored them. She wiped at the tears on her cheeks. "I thought she was your ..." Jade's shoulders shook as her laughter escaped once again.

"My what?" Luke didn't look amused.

"Your ..." Jade wiped once more at the tears, and tried to sober. It was no use. "Wife," she blurted before once again bursting with gales of laughter.

Luke glared at their audience, then took Jade by the arm and steered her into an adjoining room, slamming the door behind them. He looked at her then, his tawny eyes smouldering. Jade found it hard to breathe normally.

"I am not now." He took a step closer to her, stretching out each word as he spoke. "Nor have I ever been."

Oh, oh. He was looking at her like he was ravenous and she was the main course. Jade backed tight against the wall, no longer laughing.

"Married."

Luke placed his large hands against the wall, one on either side of her head, and claimed her lips with his. Jade's knees turned to jelly and she had to clutch his shoulders to keep from falling.

The world around them disappeared. Jade wasn't aware of anything except his lips on hers, until she felt his fingers burning a trail along the sensitive skin on the inside of her leg.

"Mmmm," he murmured. His breath was hot against her lips. "No panties."

Jade gasped when his fingers probed her hot moistness, first with one, then two fingers. She moaned as those fingers made love to her. Her nails dug into his shoulders, and her lips burned beneath his.

She was teetering on the brink of orgasm when she heard the first scream.

Instinct took over. Jade shoved Luke with such force he landed in a very undignified heap on the floor. She stepped over him to get to the door, ignoring his blustering and the curious looks of the dancers, she raced across the room and out the door she had entered through, shifting the second she was alone.

Chapter Twenty-One

A large brown wolf crouched at the edge of the brush watching the humans through the large window. The moon shone a silvery path across the mirror surface of the lake, but the wolf was more interested in the two people still inside.

It waited.

Finally, the two people began to move across the room towards the door the others had left through. The wolf crept around the building to where it could watch the couple when they came out.

They were arguing in quiet voices. The wolf sensed the anger coming from the female and the frustration coming from the male. It wanted to skulk back into the forest and hunt elsewhere, but its hunger kept it where it was.

Finally, throwing his arms up in the air and muttering something incoherent, the male stomped over to his car, and slamming the door in anger, and sped off.

Sue watched Dave drive away and sighed. She hated it when he got so angry. Sue turned around and locked the door, jiggling the handle to make sure it locked. Sometimes the lock didn't catch. She told the owner, more than once, that he needed to get a new lock, but the owner was male and like Dave, he didn't listen to her.

Sue was almost to the bottom of the steps when she spotted the brown wolf watching her from the bushes. Having lived here all her life, Sue had no fear of the wolves which often roamed around, especially during the full moon. The people here had learned to cohabitate with the wolves, and there had never been an attack by a wolf on a human in her lifetime. As far as she knew, there had been no attacks in her grandfather's lifetime.

At the bottom of the stairs Sue took two steps towards the wolf before crouching and reaching her hand, palm up, towards the animal.

"Hello, big boy." She kept her voice quiet so she wouldn't startle him. "What are you doing out here all by yourself? Why aren't you with your friends tonight?" Sue knew quite a few wolves by sight, but this one was a stranger. Easy enough to tell, most of the wolves around here were gray wolves.

The wolf inched out of the bushes and into the open, never once taking its eyes off the female in front of it. The blood rushing in her veins called to it, and the hunger gnawed. Slowly the tip of its tail began to wag.

The way the wolf was watching her was beginning to make Sue a little nervous. Usually the wolves around here looked at her with curiosity and went away. Sometimes they would come over, sniff her hand, and let her pet their soft fur.

The wolf growled, deep in its throat, and Sue knew real fear for the first time in her life. Her first instinct was to run to her car. Common sense told her to move slowly away from the wolf.

The sour milk smell of fear was intoxicating to the wolf. It watched the woman slowly pull her arm back and begin to rise. It leapt for her throat. Sue saw the wolf jump and instinctively threw her arms up to protect her throat. Large, sharp teeth pierced her arms.

Sue screamed. Her fear and agony rang out across the lake and echoed from the hills.

*****

Luke was stunned to say the least. What had happened? One minute he had her right where he wanted her—Okay, maybe not exactly where he wanted her, which would be a place a lot more private than the mansion during a dance— the next minute she was gone, again. Only this time he was sitting on the floor like an idiot.

He brushed his pants smooth and stalked out of the mansion. The scowl on his face was enough to keep everyone at a distance. To make matters worse, he couldn't find her. Nobody had seen her after she left the mansion, which meant she had to still be on the grounds, unless she had run into the forest in her panic. Another thing he didn't understand. What had spooked her? She wasn't a virgin. Last night attested to that. Still she had acted like some outraged puritan, and taken flight.

Whatever her problem was he had to find her. It was too easy to get lost in the woods at night, or worse.

His cell phone vibrated in his pocket. "What?" he snapped irritated with the interruption.

"Luke, Daniel. You better get over to the Waterside right away."

Fear's icy fingers clutched his chest. "Talk to me Daniel?"

"Sue has been attacked."

Five minutes later he was in the parking lot of the Waterside.

"It was a wolf." The angry words reach Luke before he reached the parking lot.

"How do you know it wasn't just a dog?"

Dave glared at the crowd around them. "I know a damned wolf when I see one."

"There's no wolf around here that would attack without a good reason."

The crowd parted to allow Luke through just as Dave took a step towards the dark-haired speaker. "Are you calling me a liar?"

Blood soaked their clothing, and Sue was extremely pale and shaking, but at least she was alive. Luke stepped between the two angry men. "I'm sure nobody is calling anybody a liar," he said. He tipped his head slightly towards the dark-haired boy, which was enough to send the young man scurrying away.

A quick look assured him the blood on Dave was mostly Sue's or the assailant's but he couldn't be sure without a closer examination. "Can you tell me what happened, Dave?"

"She was attacked by a damned wolf," Dave said, still incensed. "It attacked for no reason."

Luke spoke in low, comforting tones. "Is that what happened, Sue?"

Sue sniffed. "A ... wolf." She lifted her head to look at him, tears running down her cheeks. "Strange."

Luke tensed. *Where was that ambulance?* "How do you mean strange?"

Sue sniffed again and someone handed her a tissue. She blew her nose, and tried to smile. It came out more of a grimace. "I am so stupid." She held her arm close to her, and her body rocked back and forth as she spoke. "I was locking up and I felt something behind me. There he was ... standing in the shadows, watching me. I'd never seen him before. He was large, with brown fur, and his eyes were really strange. They were such a pale blue, and they had a milky film over them. He looked so alone ... and scared."

She took another wipe at her tears. "I was just talking to him. I didn't do anything wrong. I always talk to the wolves. Sometimes it's like they understand me. Never before has one growled at me, let alone attacked."

Sue looked so lost and forlorn, sitting on the step with blood still dripping from her wounds. "Where was Dave when this happened?" Luke asked.

"That's none of your business." Dave glared at Luke.

Sue put a hand on Dave's arm. "It's okay, Dave. It's not your fault. None of this is. I shouldn't have been foolish enough to treat a wild animal like it was a lost pet." She turned her attention back to Luke. "We were arguing and I sent Dave away."

This time when she smiled it actually reached her eyes. "Lucky for me, Dave is stubborn. If he hadn't come back when he did, I would have been wolf dinner."

Luke nodded and began to scan the road behind the crowd gathered in the parking lot. "Where the hell is that ambulance?" As if on cue, a siren blared, the crowd quickly scattered, and the ambulance pulled up in front of them.

Steven climbed out followed by a much younger version of himself. He quickly cleaned and bandaged Sue's arm then made a quick examination of Dave without touching him. He nodded almost imperceptibly towards Sue.

Luke sighed, and brushed his hand through his hair. He placed his hands on Sue's shoulders, drawing her attention to him. "The wolf that attacked you." He ignored the dawning horror in Sue's eyes and continued. "It was infected with a rare disease. There's more than a small chance you've been infected. Steven and George will take you to the Center where Dr. Hristea will examine you."

Dave jumped in between Sue and Luke, shoving Luke away from his girl. "Get away from her," he shrieked. "You aren't taking her anywhere."

Several men moved towards them, but Luke raised a hand and they stopped. "Were you bitten?" he asked Dave curtly. He had never really liked Dave, and had only tolerated him for Sue's sake.

Dave stared at the blood on his sleeve in horror, seeming to notice it for the first time. His voice suddenly small, he stammered. "I don't think so."

Luke turned to George. "Hey George glad you could help out tonight. Would you take Dave to the ambulance? He needs to be tested."

"No problem, boss."

Sue and a very subdued Dave were taken to the waiting ambulance. Luke quickly rounded up a hunting party, and sent everyone else home. The ambulance pulled onto the road, and the hunting party entered the woods on the trail of the wolf.

Chapter Twenty-Two

The woods were crawling with wolves and humans alike, all looking for signs of the wolf. Jade sat on a fallen tree and put her head in her hands. Twigs snapped under careless feet. An owl screeched and flew off. Crickets chirped merrily. The canopy of the trees blocked the moon making the woods extremely dark, except for crisscrossing beams of the searcher's flashlights.

This was useless. Jade was never going to find him like this. By now the humans, in their misguided attempt to be helpful, had destroyed any clear trail left by the wolf.

Jade closed her eyes, took several deep, anchoring breaths, and let her mind search. There was something ahead, moving furtively amongst the trees. Hunger, frustration, and fear pelted her. Her skin grew clammy and her limbs began to shake. Her breath came in painful gulps. Her eyes popped open and Jade fell to the ground on all fours, quickly leaving the other's behind.

A twig snapped on the right. The white wolf paused, and listened. When no other sound came, it lifted its head and sniffed the night air. Its prey still lay ahead, so that isn't what made the noise. The wolf stood still, barely breathing, and then heard it again.

Something was moving in the same direction as she was. Whatever it was, it stayed downwind so she caught no scent. She didn't worry about whatever it was catching her scent. While in animal form she carried none. It was a strange phenomenon. One that made it easier to hunt without being detected, but sometimes it made her feel like she didn't really exist. Like the animal part of her was a dream, or the fantasy of a broken mind.

Closing her eyes, she once again reached out to her surroundings. The forest was suddenly silent. It was like the forest knew there were hunters out and didn't want to distract them. Even the breeze stilled. There were at least four wolves hunting the same prey. They were to her right, about a quarter mile behind, so they couldn't have made the sound.

With a little more concentration she found it. A raccoon. It had been in search of its dinner when it caught a whiff of the wolves. Self-preservation overrode hunger and it had found a hiding place up a nearby tree. It had snapped a twig in its haste to get out of their path. It was comfortable in its hole and would wait until the wolves had passed by before coming down and continuing on its own journey.

The hunger and frustration was growing in the hunted. The forest animals sensed it and kept silent. Jade quickened her pace, closing in. Pain and torment tore at her mind, threatening to shatter it like the mind which screamed its agony.

Jade emerged from the forest into the open area of a public campground. A bright light stood like a beacon outside the washrooms. A few campfires still flickered, but most were no more than embers or cooling ash.

A door creaked, and Jade spotted movement in the shadows next to the building where the circle of light couldn't quite reach. A young girl stepped out of the building and the door slammed shut behind her. The shadows moved until a fully-grown wolf stood between the girl and Jade.

The girl froze. This was her first time out of the city. She had been so nervous about coming here, but her friends had wanted her to come, and her mother didn't. It was supposed to be their last hurrah before starting their jobs and their new lives as adults.

Life after high school. There had been times when Samantha hadn't believed it would ever happen. That was her name, although her friends called her Sam or Sammy. It drove her mother crazy. "Why do they insist on calling you by those awful names? You are Samantha, and don't you forget it."

Samantha gave a mental shrug. It really didn't matter anymore what her friends called her. Her mom, as always, would have the last say and there was no doubt in Sam's mind what she would have put on her tombstone. Her full name, Samantha Annabelle Wilson. God how she had hated that name. Now, because of a cruel twist of fate, she would suffer eternity lying beneath a stone which bore that dreadful name. Along with, no doubt, something like ... The girl never did listen.

Well Mom, you were right, as usual. I should never have come on this trip. Looks like I won't be coming home.

Samantha wondered if it would be quick. Would the wolf kill her instantly, or toy with her first. She really hoped it would be quick. She hated pain. Sam knew she should run, or scream for help. That's it. Maybe if she screamed loud enough she could scare the wolf off.

She stared into those pale blue eyes – eyes that looked almost human – and her throat constricted until no sound could escape. She tried to run, but her legs wouldn't move. She told them to, she begged them to, but they were a lot like the rest of her. They didn't listen.

Sam closed her eyes and prayed it would be quick.

The wolf hunched between Jade and the camper, its back to Jade. Hunger rose from it in waves. The girl was frozen by her fear, unable to move on her own. The tip of the wolf's tail began to twitch signalling its intention to attack, and it growled low in its throat. The sound didn't carry, but Jade felt it.

Jade leapt into the air, shifting into owl form in a single heartbeat. *Run!* Her mind shoved the command into the girl's.

Sam suddenly found her body responding and she rushed past the wolf without slowing down or turning to see if it had followed. Once she had reached the relative safety of her tent, she crawled into her sleeping bag, pulled it up over her head, closed her eyes, and prayed for morning.

The girl rushed past. The wolf pounced, only to howl its frustration when it caught empty air and rolled to the ground. Scrambling to its feet it began to chase its prey. The owl screeched a warning seconds before it slammed into the wolf, knocking it off its feet. Its prey forgotten, the wolf now fought to protect itself. The owl swooped repeatedly, ripping flesh and fur with each attack. The wolf howled in pain and frustration.

Jade shifted into wolf form and pounced. Shouting distracted Jade, and the brown wolf struck. Razor sharp teeth sank into fur and flesh. Crimson rivers ran over snow-white fur. Jade shook the other wolf off, knocking him to the ground. Her powerful jaws found their target, and snapped the brown wolf's neck.

There was a low growl behind her. Jade spun around to stare into the yellow eyes of a huge gray wolf. There was something heart wrenchingly familiar about those eyes. There was a slight movement to her left, and Jade realized they weren't alone. Three others were attempting to circle her. Jade had never run from a fight before, but these wolves had done nothing to warrant their deaths.

The white wolf tipped its nose in an almost imperceptible nod towards the gray wolf with the yellow eyes and leapt into the air.

The white owl circled them once before disappearing over the treetops.

Chapter Twenty-Three

Moarté. Luke had known she was here, but he didn't have to like it. Would she leave now that she had dealt with the killer? Not likely. They had interrupted her before she was finished. She wouldn't leave without satisfying herself that she had destroyed the mongrel. Luke hadn't recognized the wolf. It wasn't one of his. But it was of his blood. Of that he was positive. He could smell it.

This wasn't over yet. Not by a long shot. He offered up a silent prayer that for once in his life he was wrong.

There was a shimmer of magic and Luke, Daniel, Grégoire, and young Greg stood in a circle around the brown wolf. Daniel knelt beside the body and felt for a pulse.

"He's alive."

Luke turned towards the man approaching, his shotgun dangling from his arm at his side, and gave a curt nod. The sour milk scent of fear permeated the air, but other than the wary gray eyes, the man showed no other outward signs of his discomfort. Luke had the utmost respect for the man able to conquer his fear and face the four of them.

"Evening, Jack," he said casually.

The man inclined his own head slightly in acknowledgement of the other men. "Luke," he answered. He took a handkerchief from his pocket and swiped at the sweat now beading on his forehead. Luke noticed the shift of the shotgun, putting it into trembling fingers.

Jack cleared his throat and pointed the tip of the gun at the wolf, lying in a steadily increasing pool of blood, its head at an awkward angle. "One of yours?"

"No." Luke turned his attention to the body lying on the ground. "We'll need shovels and a couple of trucks."

Jack gave a quick nod. "No problem. I'll send the boys out to help."

Luke was staring at the body, but he was seeing a white wolf with one of a kind amber eyes, and a scent he would never forget. He shook his head to clear away the image. "We'll handle it," he said, his voice edged in anger. "Can't risk anyone else getting infected."

Jack shuddered. "Who?" was all he said.

Luke ignored the question. Jack knew enough about them as it was. "Where are the trucks," he asked instead.

"Behind the office. Keys are in them. Shovels are in the shed." Wary gray eyes glanced again at the body. "I didn't aim at them."

No, he hadn't. If he had, at least one—if not both—would be dead. Jack wasn't known for missing a target, moving or otherwise. "I know, Jack."

Jack returned to the office. Daniel and his son collected the trucks and shovels. With more care than required they placed the mongrel in one to be taken to the clinic. The other they loaded with tainted soil.

Chapter Twenty-Four

The owl flew drunkenly across the sky, coming to land in a large maple outside the window Jade had left open earlier. She took a second to make sure there was nobody lurking around, and then slipped into her room. Dropping silently to the floor, she shifted. Fire tore through her side where the other wolf had bitten her.

Undressing as she went, Jade entered the small, adjoining bathroom and stepped into the shower. Reaching for the faucet brought with it another bout of excruciating pain. It felt like a dozen sharp teeth were once again tearing into her flesh. While the water sprayed its own brand of stinging needles across her skin, Jade examined the wound. The long, red tendrils snaking out from the already healing wound had her worried.

Jade stayed in the shower until most of the soreness left her body, and the water began to cool. Reluctantly she left the shower, and wrapped herself in one of the thick, terry towels hanging on a hook. She needed sleep, but first she needed something to help with her bruises. Shifting may heal broken bones but Jade needed rest to recoup her strength. Rest denied to her at the moment. The Lycan gene was already trying to adhere itself to her own DNA. She could feel her blood fighting it. She needed to use the connection to Sue before it was gone. The shared wolf's blood.

"Damn!" There wasn't enough goldenseal to make a poultice to cover her bruises. She would have to restock as soon as possible. Right now she needed to concentrate on Sue, and getting her through what was coming.

She pulled the covers up to her chin, and still her body shivered uncontrollably. She considered starting the fire, but was afraid she wouldn't be able to control the magic and might burn down the house. The distance across the room was much too far to reach on foot. A slight creak brought her attention to Charlotte Gray, who was standing beside her bed holding a tray. A faint, calming aroma teased the corners of her foggy brain, but was soon shoved aside by the succulent aroma of venison.

Jade struggle to sit, cringing at the sudden stabbing in her side. Mrs Gray set the tray on the bedside table and helped her, then fluffed the pillow, all the while clucking like a mother hen. "You left in such a hurry earlier you didn't get your tea," she scolded.

"Thanks, Mrs G." Jade took a sip of the offered cup and immediately her body began to relax. *How did you get in here?*

Mrs G knew she was back? Had she locked the door? Of course she had. She locked it when she left to ensure it would be empty if she had to return in a hurry. Did she unlock it? Had she started to go down to the kitchen for something and changed her mind? Jade gave her head a mental shake to rid it of the jumbled thoughts. It didn't really matter now anyway.

She bit into the sandwich, savouring the spicy meat. "This is good," she mumbled, her mouth full.

Mrs Gray smiled and busied herself straightening the blankets around Jade. Then she picked up the wet towel from the floor where Jade had let it drop.

"You don't need to do that Mrs G." Jade made a move to get out of bed when another stabbing pain laid her back.

"There, there, Miss Jade." Mrs Gray was suddenly there, gently laying Jade back against the fluffed up pillows. "You just drink your tea and let me do what I need to do." She handed Jade the cup as she spoke, and stood there waiting.

Jade was beginning to feel like a naughty child under her scrutiny, so she drank every drop of the tea. There was something familiar and comforting about the tea. Jade handed the empty cup to Mrs Gray. "Thanks," she murmured. Her eyelids were growing heavy and she let herself slip back down under the covers. *Mullen!*

She struggled to sit up, but it was like trying to swim in quick sand. "You drugged me," she accused, as she slipped into unconsciousness.

The doorbell chimed. Mrs Gray patted the covers smooth around Jade's shoulders. "Don't you worry Miss Jade. Nobody will be bothering you tonight. You just rest and let yourself heal."

Jade didn't hear the shutting of the door or the clicking of the lock.

*****

"I demand to see her. Now!" Luke pulled himself to his full height, towering over Charlotte Gray, and glared at her. She wasn't the least bit intimidated by him, and that made him even angrier than he already was. How could he have not known who, and what, she was?

"Sit down Lykos. And quit glaring at me like I'm the enemy. I'm not. And neither is that woman upstairs."

"So you admit she is here?" He was already heading for the hall when he found himself sprawled in the nearest kitchen chair.

"I said sit down." Mrs Gray's voice thundered in the silence of the house. "Do Not made me eject you from this house."

Luke's first instinct was to break the invisible restraints holding him in place. Upon reflection, he took a deep breath, brushed his hand through his hair, and forced himself to visibly relax.

"Point taken," he muttered in a much more amenable tone. The restraints were lifted, but he stayed in his seat. He may have been making a fool of himself, but he was no fool.

"Glad to see you've come to your senses." Charlotte poured a cup of tea from the ever present pot on the stove, and set it in front of Luke. "They're bringing the girl tonight. I've readied the room."

Luke cringed. Sue would go through hell in the next few hours. If she were strong enough—and lucky enough—she would make it through alive. Then, if she learned to control the wolf she would return to her family, a very different person. If not. Luke didn't even want to think about what he would have to do if that happened. The same way he didn't want to think about what he had to do once they got the DNA results from the dead wolf.

"She can't stay."

Charlotte's eyes expressed her sympathy and understanding. "She stays. And I hope I don't have to remind you that as long as she does she is under my protection."

Luke glanced up when Charlotte's small hand covered his own larger one. "It'll be okay, Lykos," she told him.

Luke's own eyes were shadowed with fear and worry. "You know, don't you?"

Charlotte smiled, a sad knowing smile, and shrugged. "They're here," she said.

The bell hadn't rung, and Luke hadn't heard a sound, but Charlotte opened the door and let Steven in, followed by two young men carrying a stretcher. Sue lay on the stretcher. Her face peaceful in sleep. Luke wished it could stay that way, but it wasn't to be. Even those born with the Lycan gene had a hard time during the first few changes. And they had family and friends to help them prepare for what was to come. Sue didn't have the luxury of preparing for what was about to happen to her.

"Steven?"

Steven's black eyes were so full of pity Luke knew what he was going to say before he opened his mouth. "We need to talk, Lykos."

No! This couldn't be happening again. What cruel trick were the Fates playing on him now? Hadn't Gheorgès been enough? Luke didn't think he would survive losing any more family.

Chapter Twenty-Five

The sun shone brightly above the Inner Sanctum. In the room below two men sat on the floor watching the girl as she slept on the mattress. There was no bed. There was no other furniture of any kind. Just the mattress. At least four inches of foam and leather padded the floor, and walls. The only light came from three fluorescent bulbs recessed in the ceiling and protected by metal grates. It was a padded cell, created to keep its occupants from hurting themselves.

The sedative Elizabeth had administered was wearing off, and Sue stirred. Luke sprang to his feet, and approached the mattress. "Hello Sue. How are you feeling?"

Sue blinked several times before finally focusing on his features. "Mr Wulfson?" Her voice was a dry rasp. She tried to grin but it disappeared almost as soon as it started, and her eyes blurred with pain. "Who's making that racket? Can't you make them stop?" she complained.

Luke placed his hand on Sue's forehead. It was on fire. *Randy, would you go get something for our patient to eat?*

"Do you need to yell?" complained Sue, tears in both her voice and her eyes. "It's bad enough they are drilling inside my head."

Luke stared at Sue in shock, and disbelief. She shouldn't have been able to hear his thoughts. It was much too soon. Her powers were developing quicker than he imagined possible. She must be a powerful psychic. That would help her through the transformation. He just hoped it would be enough.

"We will try and be quieter," he told her, his voice barely above a whisper.

Thanks. Her eyes drifted shut, and she fell back into an uneasy slumber.

Luke took his position on the floor, while Randy went in search of food. It was going to be a very long day.

*****

Upstairs the tea began to wear off, and Jade began to stir. The pain in her side was less considerable, but her mind was still far from clear.

"How are you feeling?" The voice was familiar, and comforting.

Jade's eyes flicked open and it took several seconds for her to focus on her surroundings. As she struggled to sit up, Mrs Gray put her tray on the bedside table, and reached out to help her.

Jade pushed the woman's hands away and tried to glare, but that only caused ice picks to pierce her brain. "You drugged me," she accused. She hated that her voice came out whiny instead of firm and imposing.

"Now Miss Jade. I would never do such a thing. I would never harm a soul in this house."

Jade wanted to believe her, but there was a little thing stopping her, like drugged tea.

"You needed rest to help you heal. I just gave you a nice cup of mullein tea to help you along." She held her hands out with the palms up to indicate she was harmless, then turned them down and shook them. "See. No tricks up my sleeve."

Jade really wanted to believe the woman. She *had* needed rest, and the tea *had* helped. If the truth was known, she could use another day of sleep, but she had a job to finish. First she had to find out if she had killed the wolf, and then she had to find out what had happened to it. The wolf was feral and acting on instinct alone. Had something happened to shatter its psyche or was it newly turned? If recently turned, why allowed its freedom in such a state? Perhaps it was a mongrel. If so, had he been born with the gene? Thoughts ran rampant through Jade's restless mind. Their laws were strict. No established pack would allow such a thing to happen. So what had happened? It was up to Jade to discover what had happened, and what action was warranted. She was going to need that body. Thoughts of the wolf turned to thoughts of Sue. She should have been able to connect with the girl last night. Had the tea fuddled her so much, or was something else going on. She forced herself to focus on Mrs Gray.

"What's on your tray today, Mrs G?"

Mrs Gray's lips widened in a large smile, and her blue eyes sparkled. "Today I have brought you steak and eggs, and a nice cup of mullein tea."

Drool was already forming at the corners of Jade's mouth. "Now that you mention it, I am a little hungry." Starving was more like it. Her stomach growled in response to the mouth watering aroma when Mrs Gray lifted the lid from the tray. She gave Mrs Gray a lopsided grin, and shrugged. "Okay. I admit it. I'm starving."

She devoured the steaks and eggs, and willingly drank the mullein tea. Her senses told her there was nothing extra in it this time and she did need the rest. The tea would help her relax. With heavy eyelids she once again slid under the covers. A faint smile touched her lips, as Mrs Gray tucked the blankets around her shoulders.

Chapter Twenty-Six

"Let your body relax. Don't try to fight it. Embrace it. You will find it much easier that way."

The voice came through the fog, distant and distorted. Like someone talking with their mouth full of cotton balls. Still she recognized the deep timber in that voice.

"What's happening to me?" The other voice quivered on the verge of tears. *Somebody help me.* There was so much pain and fear in that silent plea it tore at Jade's soul.

Where are you? Jade tried to find the source of the voice but couldn't navigate through the fog in her own brain.

Who are you? It was a timid voice. Timid and painfully familiar.

She was close. He was close. Too close. Jade couldn't risk exposure. Not now. Not until she was sure the girl was safe. She jumped when she heard his voice again.

"Who are you talking to?" He was demanding in his quiet, forceful way.

Jade would have to be extra careful. He was too close. Why was she hearing his voice? Through the girl? It had to be. She had fully connected with the girl. She didn't dare alert him. *Don't tell him*, she warned. *Look around. Do you know where you are?*

"Nobody." Sue looked at Luke like he was crazy. "I didn't say anything." She looked around the room, at the padded walls and padded floor, up at the bright fluorescent bulbs, then back at Luke, allowing Jade to see everything she saw. "You must be hearing things," she said. "I don't see anyone here."

That's good. Don't tell him I'm listening, Jade told the girl.

Tell him? Who? Mr Wulfson? What would I tell him? That I am having a conversation in my head with a stranger? Wow! I am having a conversation in my head with a stranger, aren't I? How is that possible? Oh crap. I must be going crazy.

Jade's laughter was cut short by Sue's scream, as the pain ripped her muscles apart. Sue's brain began to shut down, and she went into convulsions. Jade quickly wrapped Sue's fragile brain in a cocoon, and drew Sue's pain into herself.

Sue's body quit twitching and she lay quietly, no longer aware of anything going on around her, or within her. She never felt Luke's gentle touch as he checked for a pulse, or heard his gentle, encouraging voice as he replaced the dry cloth on her forehead with a fresh cool one.

In the room two floors above Jade's body began to convulse with such violence her bed actually rattled against the floor. Her own body, already weakened from the poison in her veins, was almost incapable of holding on to Sue's pain. Stubbornly she clung to it, determined that Sue would survive.

The door to her room burst open, and Mrs Gray flew in. She grabbed Jade by the shoulders, and tried to hold her steady. "Open your eyes," she demanded.

Go away, Jade pushed at the voice trying to break her concentration.

"You cannot do this. Let her go," the voice insisted.

Need to help, Jade whimpered. She had no strength to converse. The strain of trying to hold on was wearing her down, and the voice wouldn't go away. Both bodies twitched, once, then twice, and then stilled. The first battle had been won.

Jade didn't open her eyes. She welcomed oblivion with open arms.

*****

Luke checked Sue's pulse. It was weak, and steady. Her breathing was shallow, but strong. That was good. She needed her rest. She was going to need all the strength she could muster before the coming night was over.

"I'm starving."

Luke jumped to his feet. Sue was sitting up, her back against the wall, and her eyes were bright with fever. She offered Luke a half-hearted grin.

"How long have I been asleep?"

Luke looked up at the ceiling. The moon was beginning to rise. He could feel the strength of his own powers rising with it. "Most of the day."

"You're joking. Right? I never sleep in." She looked around at the padded walls, and shifted uncomfortably on the mattress. "Where am I?"

"How are you feeling?" Luke asked.

"Exhausted. Hungry. Like I got in the way of the liquor delivery truck."

"Do you remember anything that happened?" Luke watched Sue closely as she struggled to remember. He gathered more from her chaotic thoughts, than from her actual words.

"I was closing the bar. Dave and I were arguing, and I sent him home." She tipped her head back to gaze at the bulbs in the ceiling, and chewed on her lower lip. "There was a wolf."

Her eyes widened in shock. "Oh my god. It attacked me."
She shuddered. "If Dave hadn't come back. If he hadn't
rammed it with his truck. I'd be dead right now." She stared
at the arm which showed only faint scars where open wounds
should be. She rubbed at the skin, and looked at Luke, the
question clear in her eyes. "How is that possible? There was
so much blood."

Her eyes widened in fear and she frantically searched
the room. "Why am I here? Where is Dave? He's alive, isn't
he? He didn't get hurt did he? Why can't I remember."

"Dave is fine. You on the other hand, were infected when
the wolf bit you."

"Infected? With what? Did it have rabies or something?"

Luke brushed his hand through his hair and faked
interest in the ceiling while he tried to figure out how to
explain this.

"Am I going to die, Mr Wulfson?"

Her voice was so fearful and childlike. Luke fell to his
knees beside the mattress and caught both her hands in his.
He looked her straight in the eyes. "Not if I can help it," he
promised. He knew it didn't go a long way towards making
her feel any better, but it was all he could do.

There was a rap at the door and Randy entered with a
tray. The tantalizing aroma of bear reached Luke and his
mouth began to water. His stomach growled, and he realized
he hadn't eaten since Mrs Gray's sandwiches the night
before.

"Ew. What is that horrible smell?" Sue wrinkled her
nose is disgust.

When both Randy and Luke gaped at her, she turned
bright pink. "Oh. I'm sorry. That was awfully rude of me. I
hope I didn't offend you. Randy, isn't it?"

Randy nodded but kept his eyes on the floor in front of
him.

"I am sorry, Randy. I hope you didn't think I meant you."
She sniffed the air, and grinned. "Actually, you smell rather

good. I meant the food. I can't stand the smell of meat. I'm a vegetarian."

Things keep getting better and better, thought Luke. "Maybe we can dig up a salad for you," he suggested.

Randy thrust the tray at Luke and hurried out the door, eager to please their guest. *Looks like Randy won't be making puppy dog eyes at my sister anymore.* He turned his attention back to Sue who was busy examining the wall where Randy had just disappeared.

"Something bothering you?" he asked.

"I was just wondering how Randy opened the door," Sue said. "I don't see any doorknob, or any lever."

Luke winked at Sue, and smiled. "Don't worry. We'll open the door in the case of an emergency."

The aroma from the tray in his hands was torture. His stomach growled again, and Sue actually laughed at him.

"Sounds to me, like you're a little hungry yourself."

Luke felt foolish holding a tray of food with his mouth watering in anticipation, and his stomach growling in frustration. If he was alone he would have already devoured every morsel. Instead he sat it in the farthest corner, and sat down beside the mattress to wait for Sue's salad to arrive.
*****

Upstairs, Jade woke to find a tray on the bedside table. She used the bathroom, and had a quick shower. The wound in her side was almost healed, but her ribs were bruised, and painful. She returned to the bed, ate the two sandwiches made with thick slabs of homemade bread, and even thicker slabs of bear roast.

Returning to the bathroom she dumped the tea down the drain and filled the cup with cool water from the tap. Ten minutes later she was sleeping peacefully.

Chapter Twenty Seven

"Why am I here and not in a hospital?"

Sue had enjoyed her meal of fresh fruits and vegetables, but the aroma from Luke's plate of bear roast and gravy had actually started to smell good. She wiped her mouth on the napkin provided, and set it on the tray with the empty dishes. On cue, the door swung open and Randy entered to collect the trays and dishes. He had changed into a clean pair of jeans, and a white button-up shirt.

"You must be psychic," Sue teased. She faked a cough to hide the bubbly laughter when he turned bright pink. He moved gracefully, for a man of his size, and spinning around he left the room without saying a word.

Sue shivered, and began rubbing her arms vigorously. "It feels like ants crawling under my skin," she complained.

"How's the head?"

Sue put her hands up, and gently patted her head in several places. "Wow!" she said. "I can't believe it's still in one piece."

Luke's laughter rumbled in the small room. Sue relaxed against the wall. "Okay, Mr Wulfson. I think it's time you levelled with me. Just how serious is this, and what are my odds?"

"You were infected by a rare ... virus ... when you were bitten so you have been quarantined."

"Quarantine I understand, but a padded cell? Do you expect me to go mad and try to hurt myself?" Her eyes widened. "I am going to go mad, aren't I? In fact it has already started."

"I won't lie to you. It happens. But I have a feeling that it isn't going to happen to you."

Sue pulled her legs up to her chest, wrapped her arms around them, and began rocking. "Then why?" Sue began, and then decided not to mention the conversation in her head. After all, she wasn't even sure it had actually happened. If it did happen, that was strange she would admit, but if it didn't happen, then that meant she was going crazy. Crazy wasn't something she was planning to do well.

"Why what?"

The way Mr Wulfson was looking at her, like he was trying to read her mind, scared her. She could almost feel something moving around inside there, searching. For what, she didn't know. "Nothing," she mumbled. "I must have been dreaming."

"Not everyone goes mad."

He wasn't very convincing. "If I don't go crazy, what does happen to me?"

"If you don't go mad, you learn to live with it."

"And what is it, exactly?"

Luke seemed very uncomfortable. He tried to loosen the collar on his t-shirt while feigning interest in the ceiling, again. He began to speak just as Sue was beginning to think that he wouldn't answer her.

"You have been infected with the Lycan gene. It is passed through saliva, and blood."

"Like aids?"

"Somewhat, yes."

"Dave was covered with blood."

"True. He has already been tested and sent home. He doesn't have it."

"I do."

"Yes, Sue. You do."

"Is it fatal?" She may as well get rid of the big worries first. After all, if she were going to die, the rest didn't really matter anyway.

"Rarely."

So far so good. "Will my hair fall out?"

"If it does, I can personally guarantee that it will grow back," he teased.

Sue quit rocking and offered Luke a weak smile. "I'm ready to listen. Tell me exactly what to expect. Forewarned is forearmed, my Grandpa always says."

Luke took a deep breath and expelled it very slowly. "The Lycan gene is carried in the saliva and blood. When a human is bitten, the gene travels through their blood bonding with their own DNA and changing it. The person becomes two joint, but separate beings. A human that can shape-shift into a wolf."

Sue laughed, but she wasn't exactly sure that the man telling the story didn't believe it himself. He couldn't be serious. Werewolves? That was ridiculous. Wasn't it? *That is ridiculous, isn't it?* She asked the voice in her head, but it was silent. She asked the man in the room instead.

"A werewolf?" She shook her head. This was unbelievable. "You don't actually believe in werewolves, do you?"

"We are Lycan, not werewolf."

His serious expression scared her. He couldn't actually believe what he was telling her. "You're nuts."

Sue started to rise from her place on the mattress but Luke's steady gaze held her in place. "You are serious. You do actually believe what you are saying." She looked towards the wall where she knew the door should be. If only Randy were to walk through that door right now.

"I am serious, Sue. And no matter how hard you look, nobody is going to come in here and save you from me."

Oh! What was he doing now, reading her mind? "Okay." Maybe she could trick him into opening the door. He did say he could from in here. She would ask to see a werewolf. Then when he opened the door to go find one, she would escape. "If werewolves exist, prove it. Go find me one."

The words were no sooner spoken when Luke shimmered, and a large gray wolf squatted in his place. Sue's screams bounced off the walls, and just as quickly the wolf became Luke.

"How? How did you do that?" Sue stammered.

"I was born Lycan. I have had centuries to perfect the change."

Sue eyed him a little more warily than before. She had been born in Willow Bend, and thought she knew everyone. Apparently, she didn't know Mr Wulfson all that well. Then again, maybe she did? Maybe he was exactly who she had believed him to be her whole life. Maybe she was already crazy. That was it. She was already crazy. If so, what did she have to lose? She'd just play along.

"How old are you?"

"Let's just say I'm a bit older than you." *Quite a bit older.*

You could say that again. He had to be at least forty. "If I'm a werewolf, can I do that?"

Luke grinned, baring his teeth, which suddenly looked a whole lot larger than before. "As leader of the pack it is my duty to teach you."

"There's a pack? Cool. How many?" Sue gave herself a mental shake. Way to go, stupid. Like that is the most important thing he said.

"Let's just say, this is my town."

Sue cried out, and doubled over clutching her stomach. It felt like something was trying to tear its way out. "What's happening?"

"The moon is rising. With the rising of the moon, your powers will increase tenfold. With the rising of the full moon comes the change. Later, when you are stronger, you may be able to control when you change. I can change at will. I am able to stop the change at will. Many never get strong enough to stop the change during the full moon."

She watched as he reached behind his neck and removed a chain with a small medallion, placing it around her own neck. Then he put his arms around her, and gently rocked her. His voice was hypnotic, lulling Sue into a false sense of security, and she began to relax. As she relaxed, the pain subsided.

He lifted her hand to the medallion. "Take it," he told her. "Rub it between your fingers. Envision the wolf. Become one with the beast."

Sue's limbs began to shake, bend, and twist. She tried to stop them, but it only made the pain worse. The first bone snapped. She screamed. A million tiny needles pricked her skin as hair thrust through. Her clothes began to tear as her body warped and grew.

Through it all she could hear his voice. "Don't fight it Sue. Embrace your inner beast. Become one with the wolf."

Her screams became vicious growls as a hundred and twenty pound brown wolf, with gray around its collar and forepaws, rose to its feet and faced Luke. The wolf snarled and snapped at the human in front of it. Instead of cringing in fear, or fleeing, the human stood and faced the young wolf, stretching itself to an impressive height.

The young wolf was wary of this human who showed no fear. Its eyes darted from side to side, frantically searching for a means of escape. With no escape in sight, the wolf's instinct was to attack. Growling low in its throat it advanced slowly, the tip of its tail twitching in warning.

There was a shimmer and a two-hundred-pound gray wolf stood in the man's place. It stood perfectly still, not a hair moving, and stared at the younger, smaller wolf.

The younger wolf's growls turned to whimpers, and it cowered with its back to the wall.

Chapter Twenty Eight

Moonbeams streamed through the open window, teasing Jade to wakefulness. The soreness in her ribs was almost completely gone, and there was no trace of a bite. Jade jumped out of bed and stretched, letting the moon's magic caress her, chasing away the last of her small aches and pains.

She put on clean, olive cargo pants and a tan sweater. She pulled a pair of clean socks out of her pack, and a small paper fluttered to the floor. Jade picked it up, and found herself staring into two of the blackest, saddest eyes she had ever seen. She couldn't believe it had only been a couple of days since she left Alicia at the airport. She hoped she was settling in okay. If anyone could pull the child out of her shell, Da could.

Jade carefully refolded the picture and returned it to her pack, put on her socks and hiking shoes, and went downstairs in search of food. When she entered the kitchen, Mrs Gray was busy piling food onto a plate. "Hello dear. Sleep well?"

Jade smiled brightly. "Like a log," she replied. "Thanks for everything, Mrs G."

Mrs Gray's head bobbed and she clucked her tongue. "Just doing what anyone else would. I'm sorry the chamomile tea wasn't to your liking."

Confused, Jade looked at her curiously.

"The tea dear. You didn't drink it with your sandwiches. I had thought that you would find the flavour soothing, but not everyone likes chamomile."

Jade vaguely remembered pouring the tea down the drain, but how on earth did Mrs Gray know about that? "It's not I don't like chamomile," Jade hedged. "I just felt like water."

Mrs Gray patted her hand in a motherly fashion, and set a plate piled high with steak, home fried potatoes, and three eggs in front of Jade. "That's okay, dear. I understand perfectly."

Jade was sure she did. Nothing seemed to get by the lady in charge of the Inner Sanctum.

Jade ate her meal in silence, savouring each bite as if she hadn't eaten for days, instead of a few hours. After sucking the marrow from the bone, she licked her fingers slowly, not wanting to waste a single drop of the spicy goodness. If only she could cook like that.

She wiped her face and fingers on a napkin, placed it on her plate, and slid the whole thing forward; afraid she might be tempted to lick the plate clean. Patting her stomach she said, "Delicious."

Mrs Gray grinned, her round cheeks ruddy, and quickly cleaned the dishes.

"Did you hear what happened to Sue over at the Waterfront Bar?"

"Yes I did. The poor child."

"Do you know where they took her? I'd like to go see how she is doing. I met her and Dave last night. They seem like a very nice couple."

"Nobody can go see her. She's in quarantine."

"For a wolf bite?" Jade knew it wasn't going to be easy. Luke had her hidden somewhere and she had to find her. It wasn't that she didn't think that Sue would be safe with Luke; she just wanted to see for herself. Jade had tried to reach out to Sue when she woke up, but the connection was lost.

"They think the wolf might have been carrying some kind of disease."

"Like rabies?"

Mrs Gray gave Jade a strange look. "Something like that," she said. She suddenly remembered she had forgotten to clean one of the guest rooms, and excused herself, leaving Jade alone in the kitchen.

Jade went out but the town was unusually quiet. It was almost like they were in mourning. The humans had locked themselves in for the duration of the full moon. One of their own had been hurt, and they were not taking any more chances.

She went by the mansion, but the wolves there were subdued, eyeing her with as much suspicion as lust. She hung around for a while, but when Luke didn't show she left. Jade hadn't really expected him to show. He would be holed up somewhere with Sue. Unwanted jealousy clawed at Jade's insides, and she berated herself. What was wrong with her? She was feeling, and acting out of character and she didn't like it one little bit. For the second night in a row the males around her held no interest, even though their pheromone levels were high.

Jade went back to the sanctum of her room, and allowed her dreams of Luke to carry her into the night.

The sun was just beginning to rise. The air was still crisp this time of day, but the coming heat was evident in the first rays of the sun. It wouldn't take long before the sun rose above the surrounding trees, and then even here she wouldn't be safe from the heat.

Jade stopped near the small creek, and listened as the water trickled over stones as it race to join the lake. A babbling brook. The thought brought a slight smile to her lips. This would be the perfect spot. There were no houses nearby. Sanctuary stood tall and formidable between herself and the road. Charlotte was busy in the kitchen. Helen had left suddenly, and Randy was still in bed as far as Jade could tell.

Perfect.

Jade lifted her arms slowly, drawing air deeply into her lungs, and expelling it just as slowly as she lowered them. She did that a couple of times before swaying back and forth with them extended to stretch the muscles in her sides, before bending forward to touch her toes, and work the kinks out of her back.

Aw. She needed that. As each vertebra gently stretched before falling back into place the tension began to leave her body, and her mind began to focus. She placed her hands flat on the ground before her, and began to walk them forward until she was in a downward facing dog position. She held the position until she could feel the strain in her muscles, and then held it for a couple of minutes longer. Jumping her feet together, Jade slowly stood upright, once again raising her arms to reach for the sun. After a few more basic stretches she bent over backwards until her outstretched fingers touched the earth behind her.

The earth was cool beneath her fingers. She was at one with the earth around her. Then there were two. Jade sensed his presence. He stood down wind so she didn't catch his scent but her body knew instinctively who was there. Heat began at her core, and quickly spread.

Jade held perfectly still, focused on her breathing, and waited. Every sense reached out to him. He moved closer, and her skin tingled with electricity. She hated him for the way he made her feel. Her bones began to melt and she had to concentrate to hold her pose. He was far too distracting.

Distractions could get her killed.

With her eyes closed, Jade scanned the immediate area. Charlotte was still busy in the kitchen. Randy was in his room on the third floor just beginning to stir. She could detect no other movement in the house. That didn't mean they weren't there. She was actually surprised that she knew where Randy and Charlotte were at this moment. The enchantment on the building was there to keep the occupants safe, and prying minds out.

A squirrel eyed her warily from a tree a couple of yards away, and a small bird burst from a nearby bush.

He was mere inches from her feet.

In one continuous, fluid movement Jade swung her foot out, caught Luke by the ankle, and dropped him to the ground. She flipped her body up and over, and balanced on her toes ready to move. Luke started to stand, and Jade swung her foot out to perform a near perfect round house kick, and knocked him on his backside again. This time she pounced on him, her arm across his neck.

Jade knew he wouldn't take this lying down. She waited, tensed, readying herself for his next move, her skin humming in response to his close proximity. She was entirely unprepared for what happened next.

Luke ignored her arm against his throat. He moved his hands to her waist, and tickled. Jade burst into laughter, and attempted to push his hands away. Luke took advantage of her unsteadiness, flipped her over onto her back, and covered her body with his.

Heat flared between them.

This was so not good. Jade had never reacted to a man like this. Not even during the moon cycle. Her first instinct was to buck him off, and run. She reached up, and placing her hands on the sides of his face she pulled him closer until their lips met.

Musk filled the air around them. The scent of his arousal nurtured hers, and she groaned beneath the onslaught of his kisses. When his teeth scraped against her lower lip, she opened to the invasion of his tongue. Desire roared to life like an angry beast. With a thought, neither was sure whose; their clothes vanished leaving them skin to skin. With hungry hands they explored each other's bodies.

Luke was possessed with the need to mark her, to claim her as his own, so that the entire world would know. It didn't make any sense. Unable to control the rising need Luke spread Jade's legs and impaled her, at the same moment he sank his canines into her shoulder, and held her writhing body still as he released his seed into her.

His scent, musky campfire and spices surrounded her; entered her; marked her.

Chapter Twenty Nine

The taxi turned down another dirt road, bouncing over the rutted path. Jade's knuckles were white, but she didn't loosen her grip on the bar in front of her. *What is this the Indy 500?*

It was on the tip of her tongue to ask him to slow down yet again, when the cab came to a screeching stop. The seatbelt was the only thing keeping Jade from the front seat beside the driver.

"I should have walked," she grumbled under her breath. *Or flown.* But she would need her strength when she found the wolf so she had opted for the local taxi service. *I really need to learn to drive. I couldn't do any worse than this.*

She paid the driver, and told him not to wait. "I'm meeting a friend," she lied. "I'll get a ride back." There was no way she was getting back in a taxi with that maniac.

The driver beamed when she gave him enough to cover what would have been her return fair, and left with a squeal of tires that left her covered in dust. *Oh this is just great. I would have been cleaner walking.* Jade brushed the dust from her favourite pair of "Illegal Cargo" pants. She would have just changed into something else but suddenly the parking lot was overflowing with people.

While patting the dust from her clothes, Jade felt something in her side pocket. Distracted, she reached in and pulled out a half eaten chocolate bar. Things were definitely looking up. She peeled the paper away from the squished, melted chocolate, and popped it in her mouth. Now this was heaven. Music may soothe the savage beast, but give her chocolate anytime. She slowly licked the gooey mess from the paper, crumpled and returned it to her pocket, and turned to enter the Wolf Center.

She froze.

It was beautiful. The building was built from a combination of field stone and logs. It appeared to grow right out of the ground. A part of nature rather than a man made abode. The thatched roof blended with the trees that towered over it. Jade wasn't sure she would have been able to distinguish it from the forest from the air. If she hadn't already been impressed with the way Mr Wulfson ran his holdings, this building would have sealed the deal. Jade could look at this building all day, except she still had a job to do.

Last night the Willow Bend pack had stopped her from destroying the rogue wolf. An innocent woman was infected, and a child was threatened. Not to mention that poor girl in the park, and the man in the cabin. By every law known to *were* that beast needed to be destroyed. She knew the healing abilities of lycans and she was not leaving until she was sure the killings had stopped; even if it meant turning Luke against her. She was still having a hard time with the fact that Luke was related to the pack Alpha.

Lykos Wulfson was a legend. He had led a handful of survivors from their homeland, across the vast ocean to start their lives in a strange new land. He was well-known for dealing with his pack fairly and firmly, meting out justice when the need arose. He had personally destroyed his own brother when Gheorgès had gone on a killing spree, negating the need for the *Moarté* to intercede. Jade had to speak with the male. Normally she wouldn't bother. She should just go in, do her job, and leave. There was no reason to inform anyone that she was even there. If they didn't uphold the law, she would. Anonymity was important in her line of work. If they didn't know who you were they couldn't come after you. How many times had her aunts drilled that into her head?

Jade braced herself, and entered the front doors. The inside was even more impressive than the outside. There were stuffed wolves of every species scattered around the room. Potted trees, along with very realistic fake trees helped to create an ambiance of being in the wild. Wolves skulked among the trees making Jade feel like they were actually watching her. On closer inspection Jade realized that they were actually stuffed wolves, not artificial like she had first assumed. She couldn't stop the shiver that crawled along her spine.

Near each wolf was a plague telling a little about it. These wolves had all been a part of someone's family. They had names, and history, and came from around the world. There were a couple of Iberian wolves from Spain, Alejandro and Amada, and wolves from Romania named Bogdana and Ciprian. There were Lobo, or Mexican wolves, the list went on and on. Jade pulled her attention away from the exhibit to take in her surroundings. The fourth wall was glass, and overlooked the compound where Jade could see a pair of wolves indulgently looking on while their pups romped.

Above her head Jade could hear the murmur of voices, and the shuffling of feet. That would be the main offices, and where she would find Lykos Wulfson. She glanced at the clock above the receptionist's desk, and hurried over.

"Hi." She smiled at the girl behind the desk. Although she was human, Jade could detect the lycan gene lying dormant. Jade wondered if Wulfson knew. Probably. Why else would he keep a human on here? All the other employee's wandering around were definitely lycan. "I have an appointment with Mr Wulfson."

The girl glanced at the book in front of her, and smiled. "Of course, Miss Caer. Mr Wulfson is expecting you. If you go up the stairs it's the first door on the right."

Jade thanked her, and hurried up the stairs. It was two minutes to twelve, and she really didn't want to be late. She was just about to knock on the door when she heard voices. Her hand froze.

"I need to talk to you Uncle." The voice was young, female, and very timid.

"Can't it wait, Gemma? I have an appointment." The voice was brisk, distracted, and then there was an uncomfortable silence. Jade could hear the shuffling of feet through the door. "What's wrong, Gemma?" This time the voice was much more compassionate, and held the same seductive timber she was so familiar with.

"It's." The female's voice cracked with nervousness. "Never mind. It can wait until after your appointment. Are you coming to Elizabeth's for supper tonight?"

"I was planning on it. Are you sure you don't want to tell me what's wrong. I can cancel my appointment."

Good for you, thought Jade. It gladdened her heart that the man was willing to cancel an appointment for the sake of a member of his pack.

"No. It can wait." The girl forced a brighter tone to her voice. "I'll see you tonight."

Jade rapped on the door. It swung open revealing a very young, very beautiful female. She reminded Jade of Helen. Jade extended her hand. "Hello. I'm Jade Caer. I didn't mean to interrupt, but I have an appointment with Mr Wulfson. The receptionist said to come right up."

Gemma hesitated, and then took Jade's offered hand. "I'm Gemma Radu," she said, her voice much more confident that it had been through the door.

Their hands touched and Jade felt the younger woman's pulse. She smelt the blood rushing through her veins. She tasted fear, and confusion. Jade listened to the rapid beat of Gemma's heart, and the quicker, gentler tapping of the second heartbeat. *She's pregnant.* Relief swept through Jade a mere heartbeat before the vision nearly knocked her to the floor.

She felt her sharp white teeth sink into the man's flesh. The salty tang of his warm blood hit the back of her throat in a rush.

Gemma blanched and tugged her hand free. "I was just leaving." She slurred the words like a drunk. "Uncle Luke is all yours." She slipped past Jade and pulled the door shut with a loud click.

An impatient sound came from the man behind the desk, and Jade snapped back to the present. The taste of blood lingered on her tongue. She forced her attention to the only other person in the room. *Could this day get any worse?* She wondered. "You have got to be kidding me. You are Lykos Wulfson?" Dark eyes sparkled, and Jade nearly groaned again. *Oh this cannot be happening.*

"Lykos was my great grandfather." His voice was gruff with emotion as he waved her towards an empty chair across from his desk. "I'm Luke Wulfson." He didn't offer his hand, and Jade didn't offer hers. They both knew full well what would happen should they touch. This morning had proved that.

Luke leaned back in his seat; his hands in front of him on the desk formed a tepee. He tapped his index fingers together. He appeared outwardly calm, but his insides snarled in a knot. "How can I help you Miss Caer?"

This so wasn't going to be easy. She may as well just jump right in. "Last night a woman was bitten by a wolf." Luke's eyes narrowed. Jade took a deep breath. What was it about this man that made her lose all her ability to think clearly? "I want to know what happened to the wolf." Well at least she wasn't stuttering.

"And what makes you think I'd know anything about that."

This was getting them nowhere. Jade rose and offered her hand to Luke. "Let's start over, shall we? I am Jade Caer O'Connor of O'Connor Search and Rescue."

Luke looked at her offered hand as if it were a viper about to strike. He cautiously took it in his much larger one. *Moarté!*

Jade cringed as the hated word leapt between them, and he dropped her hand like he would drop a hot poker.

"What brings you here, Miss Caer?" His voice was curt.

Jade sat back in her own chair but kept her eyes on the man in front of her. His mind had snapped shut against her the minute he realized what she was. It was inevitable the moment she sent him the knowledge. Still it hurt, which was another reason Jade usually kept the knowledge to herself. She was the dreaded *Moarté*. Born of death and destruction she killed without remorse. If only they knew the truth. She bled with every life she was required to destroy. Hers was a thankless job, that of policing the magical creatures thought to be extinct, or myth. The human police were ill equipped to deal with them, and it was Jade's job to protect all their species.

She swallowed her hurt. "A wolf killed a teenage girl in Toronto the night we met."

Those black eyes didn't flicker. *He knows,* she thought. *I wonder just how much he knows.* "I followed him here." She could hear the guilt she felt in her own voice, and took a deep breath before continuing. *I should have been out patrolling. Not having mind blowing sex with the hottest male to ever walk the planet.*

"Of course you know that," she snapped, her voice harsh. "I would have put an end to the killing last night if your wolves hadn't interfered."

Luke moved then. He slammed his hands on the desk in front of him. Rising off his chair he leaned forward, eyes snapping yellow fire, power sparking around the room. "My wolves," he snarled in barely controlled fury. "... had every right to interfere. You are on my land. I am the law here."

Wow! He is magnificent when he is angry. Jade forced her mind back to business. "You may be the law here under normal circumstances." It was funny. Now that Luke was angry Jade felt much calmer; more in control of the situation. "But the minute any *were*--Lycan, fox, eagle, it doesn't matter--Once a human is bitten it becomes our jurisdiction. I only came here today to warn you to stop interfering. That wolf is feral. Feral and blood thirsty. He will be stopped."

Luke sat back in his chair. Relief warred with some other emotion in his dark eyes. Lust? Regret? "Then you are free to go back to where ever you came from Miss Caer. The wolf died last night. Our doctor wasn't able to save him."

Jade stood. "Of course you will be able to provide proof of that."

"Of course. The body is still over at the Veterinary Hospital. Elizabeth hasn't disposed of it yet. I'll call and let her know you are on your way." Luke picked up the telephone and punched in some numbers. He spoke briefly, and hung up. "Elizabeth is busy but she will be able to see you in about an hour. That will give you time to collect your things. You can see her on your way out of town," he said hopefully.

I know you are not that stupid. Jade didn't bother to offer her hand. She knew he wasn't about to touch her again. Not now that he knew who she was and why she was here. And definitely not after he discovered she was going after his niece.

She opened the door, and left without a word or a backwards glance.

Chapter Thirty

Luke stared at the door long after Jade had left. She wasn't going to leave town. Not until after she had finished her business, and as much as he wished it wasn't true that business involved his family.

He should be angry, worried, or both. Instead he felt relief. He would be seeing her again. That scared him more than anything else.

Damn! He had to protect his family. There was no denying that the mongrel had Wulfson blood running through its veins. He had sensed it at the park, and again at the Green's house. It had been elusive, mingled with the strong residue of power, but he had suspected it. And when he faced the mongrel as he lay dying, he knew. Blood called to blood. Erzébet had run the tests three times before confirming it. If Luke hadn't turned him, and Gheorgès was long dead, that left Gemma. Luke didn't have any offspring. That boat had sailed a long time ago—with Natasha's betrayal.

Gheorgès had hated the humans, blaming them all for what a few had done to their parents, and their entire pack. Only by the grace of God, and Erzébet's help, had Luke managed to save as many of them as he had. His baby brother had only been two summers when his parents were murdered, but he had remembered every single detail of that night. It had haunted his dreams for years until he had finally snapped. He had set out to avenge his parents' deaths by destroying as many humans as possible. Unable to turn Gheorgès from his destructive path, Luke had destroyed his only brother.

Natasha's betrayal had cost him so much Luke hadn't allowed himself to feel anything for a female since. Not until a pale haired woman with glowing amber eyes.

Luke may not have been able to save his brother, but he was determined to save Gemma. Even if it meant destroying the one woman who had managed to chip the ice from his heart. Gemma was innocent. She didn't have a mean bone in her body. If she had bitten this human, then she had a very good reason, and he was determined to find out exactly what that reason was.

Tonight.

The phone rang, and Luke jumped. *Hell.* He grabbed the receiver. "This better be good," he growled into the mouth piece. He listened for a few moments. "No. Nobody talks to her. And for God's sake, keep her away from the body."

Luke replaced the phone, and smiled to himself. It wouldn't stop her but it should slow her down. At least until he had a chance to talk to Gemma. He hit another button, and waited.

"Yes, Mr. Wulfson."

"Take messages for me, Sara. I'll be out for the rest of the day."

"Yes sir. Where can you be reached in case of an emergency?"

"Call my cell if it is an emergency. But only if it is an emergency."

"Okay. Have a great day."

Luke shook his head, a half smile on his lips. "You too. And thanks Sara."

He made a mental note to give Sara a raise. She was always happy, and always willing to fit in whenever they needed her. In fact Elizabeth had told him that Sara had gone on the overnight with George this month. He'd have to remember to ask her how she liked that. Luke made it a point to try to keep up with everyone he was responsible for.

That got him thinking. Usually Gemma went out on the overnight. He was going to have to ask Elizabeth why she made the change. He should have thought of that before, but he had other things on his mind. Like a pale haired, amber eyed goddess.

Luke almost forgot to shove his cell phone in his pocket before he left the office. If he hurried he could be at the hospital before Jade. He was sure she would use conventional modes of travel, especially during the day. He, on the other hand, had no intention of using conventional methods.

He should have known better. He arrived to find an absolutely livid Elizabeth pacing outside her examining room. "What's going on?" he demanded.

"Her." Elizabeth spit out the word. "She marched in here like she owned the place. She told Ellie that she had your permission to see the body, and then ordered her out of the room." Elizabeth's dark eyes spit fire. "The stupid girl actually left her in there alone with the body. Now the door is locked and we are out here."

"Where were you when she arrived?"

"I had taken the results of the blood tests to the incinerator. I didn't know she would get here so quickly. I should have known she would not wait in case we tried to destroy the evidence. Not that it matters now."

Luke nearly laughed aloud. Not even Elizabeth could possibly know everything, and it drove her crazy. Besides, he had a feeling that nobody, not him, not Elizabeth, not anyone would have been able to keep Jade from that room.

He looked through the window. Jade was sitting cross-legged at the end of the gurney, both hands on the dead wolf's head, and her eyes closed. "What's she doing?"

Elizabeth shrugged. "Who is to know? Maybe she is asking him who he is." Luke thought she had meant it as a joke, but Elizabeth seldom joked, and she had never looked more serious. Then he felt it.

The power.

He felt compelled to look back into the room where he saw the dead wolf. Where had Jade gone? Then he noticed the shimmer of light and realized that she was still there. He watched that shimmering light for what seemed like hours, and then Jade slumped forward. He felt a lump of fear in his throat just before he heard the lock click. Luke shoved the door open and rushed to gather Jade into his arms.

She was ashen. Her skin was clammy. Her pulse was beating faster than a hummingbird's wings. *She's dying.* The thought came unbidden to his mind and he felt panic rise. "Do something, Elizabeth," he growled.

She did.

She threw a glass of ice water in Jade's face.

Jade sputtered and coughed. She struggled to sit up, but the arms holding her were warm, and safe. She settled back. *Arms!* He eyes flew open, and she found herself staring into two dark pits of worry.

"What did you do?" she snapped as she pushed away from Luke.

"He did nothing." The voice was beautiful, and commanding like the woman who possessed it.

"You must be Erzébet." Jade offered her hand but Elizabeth put her own hands behind her back. *Things were so much easier when they didn't know who she was.*

"Did you find what you need?" Elizabeth's eyes were piercing, and Jade had the feeling that she was trying to see right into her soul. Maybe she was. The woman relaxed visibly, and smiled. "Luke let the woman sit up. She is not dying this day."

Luke seemed reluctant to let her go, but he finally moved his arm from around her shoulder. Jade slid off the table, and onto the floor—in a heap. *Oh what she wouldn't give for a chocolate bar right now.* As if he had read her mind Luke reached into his shirt pocket and pulled out a granola bar.

"I don't have any candy, but this might help."

Jade took the offered energy bar, and ate it while sitting on the floor where she had landed. It was only after she had swallowed the last crumb that she realized what a vulnerable position she was in. Whether she liked it or not these people were her enemies. *Why wasn't the door locked?*

"You are safe here," Elizabeth said.

That clinches it. The woman is reaching my mind. Jade tried to throw up a mental shield, only to grab her head as two burning spears seemed to impale her. *Okay. No shields. At least not until I've gotten my strength back.*

Jade stood up with the help of the gurney, and waved off Luke's attempt to help as she staggered towards the door. "You can dispose of the body," she said. "I've seen all I need to here." In truth Jade hadn't seen what she had hoped to see, and to top it all off she had to get in another taxi.

From the instant she had touched Gemma she had known something was wrong. That girl wasn't tainted. Jade would bet her life that the child would never bite a human—except when mated. A Love Bite—that's what they called it.

Jade's heart slammed against her ribs at a flash of memory. Had Luke bitten her? No. It wasn't possible. She would know if she mated to a wolf wouldn't she? There was no battle for control going on inside of her. Of that she was positive. Could she be channelling someone else's memories?

What had happened?

Are you all right? Do you need me to come? The familiar voice brought a smile to her lips, and a glow to her face. The taxi driver looked in his rear view mirror, and nearly drove off the road. Jade clutched at the back of the front seat and glared at the driver.

Jade? The single word brought the smile back to her lips. *Do you need me to come? Are you hurt?* There was worry now in the sing-song voice.

No. I'm not hurt. Just confused. She could feel her probe. *Stop that Althea. I'm fine. I'm just trying to figure out something. How is Alicia? And Da?*

They are good. Your father dotes on the child, and she is an absolute angel. She is learning to control her powers very well for someone so young. And I have discovered that she has even more hidden talent than we first thought. Sometimes these things are buried so deep only the subconscious is aware.

Of course! Thank you. As always Althea you are a genius.

Of course! Jade heard the laughter in her voice. *How is your young man?*

Jade nearly fell off her seat, and this time it had nothing to do with the driving. *Young man?* She enquired cautiously.

The one you have gone to recruit. Her aunt's laughter spoke volumes. *I see. You will have to tell me all about this other young man when you return home. I can't wait to meet him.*

Not likely happening. Jade sighed. *Not after I'm finished here.*

The taxi came to a screeching halt at the front of Sanctuary. Jade paid the driver, and walked slowly around to the kitchen door. She couldn't ever remember when she had felt so completely exhausted. At least her aunt's short visit had reminded her that she wasn't alone. It also reminded her of her original reason for coming to Willow Bend. She had an appointment in less than an hour with Daniel Dixon at the Waterfront.

The kitchen door opened. Mrs G pulled Jade inside, and led her to a chair. "Come in child," she said. "I have a nice bowl of bear stew all ready for you."

A bell dinged, and Mrs G turned to the oven. When she opened the door the aroma of fresh bread wafted over to Jade. Her mouth began to water.

"Perfect timing," Mrs G said.

Jade couldn't have agreed more.

Chapter Thirty One

Luke studied his niece from behind his glass. Her face was too pale, and her eyes usually so full of life were haunted. It couldn't hurt worse if someone actually kicked him in the guts.

"Uncle Luke," she began. Her voice quivered.

"Not now, Gemma." Luke glanced at Elizabeth who shrugged, and gave him a probing look. She wasn't going to be any help. "Elizabeth has cooked us a wonderful meal. Let's just enjoy it. We can have our discussion later."

Gemma forced a smile that didn't quite reach her eyes. Luke couldn't tell if she was grateful for the respite or not. "I hear Sara went out on the overnight. How did she like that?" Luke sought to change the subject and was rewarded with a genuine grin from Gemma.

"She found it very interesting." Gemma pushed her food from one side of her plate to the other. The smell of it nauseated her. If she didn't tell her secret soon the guilt alone was going to eat her alive. But if Uncle Luke wanted to postpone the telling then she would have to abide by his decision. "George kissed her."

"What!"

Both Luke and Elizabeth spoke at once, and Gemma couldn't help but laugh. "George kissed her. They were arguing, again, and he just kissed her."

Luke covered his mouth and coughed to hide his laughter. What was it about Gemma that always made him laugh? He resolved to do everything in his power to save her -- even if it meant giving up his own life.

Gemma was once again pushing her food from one side of the plate to the other. She had still to take even one bite. "Is something wrong with your food?" he asked.

"Gemma ate earlier," Elizabeth volunteered, surprising them both. "She's probably not hungry."

Luke studied Elizabeth's clear eyes. *Why are you lying?* He wondered. *What do you know that I don't know?*

"Charlotte tells me that Randy is taking exceptional care of Sue," Elizabeth ventured.

Two sets of eyes turned when Gemma slammed her fork down, and shoved her plate across the table so hard that it slid off the edge, dumping her food all over the pristine floor. "It's my fault." The words burst out. "I think I turned the wolf that bit Sue. I need to be put down."

"No!" Once again Luke and Elizabeth spoke at the same time.

A small sob escaped before Gemma took a deep breath, and brought herself under control. "I was drinking. I don't remember what happened." She took another deep breath, and the words poured out." I don't know what is real anymore. I think I'm losing my mind."

Elizabeth was sitting in her chair one moment, and standing beside Gemma patting the girl's shoulder the next. "There, there child," she murmured soothingly. "Take a deep breath, let it out very slowly, and then tell us what is going on."

Once started, Gemma couldn't seem to stem the flow of words. "I have the bloodlust. I must be put down."

"Tell us why you think you have the bloodlust." Luke encouraged his niece, his gentle tone only succeeded in making her cry harder. He watched Gemma's tears flow, and his heart broke. He didn't think for one single moment that Gemma had the bloodlust. If she did, she wouldn't be sitting here so calmly telling them about it. Well, not exactly calmly. She was clearly agitated, and her eyes mirrored his confusion, but at least she was talking to them.

Ghèorges, his own brother, had lied right to the end. Even after Luke had caught him in the act, a half devoured corpse in front of him and Ghèorges covered in blood, he had denied his guilt. But Luke had seen the guilt in his eyes. For a long time he had tried to ignore what he knew to be true, but in the end he had done his duty. It had been Ghèorges or them. Luke didn't care about his own life, but his small group was all that was left of his father's pack.

Luke could detect no guilty knowledge in Gemma's eyes. There was only fear and confusion.

"It began right after I snuck out to a bar and I drank too much. I'm pretty sure there was a man there, although I don't seem to be able to remember much about that night at all. When I try to recall that night it feels like someone using a power drill on my brain." Gemma pushed her short bangs back, sighing when they fell back into place. Neither Luke nor Elizabeth spoke, waiting for the girl to continue.

"I woke up with the coppery taste of blood in my mouth." Gemma grimaced at the memory, and then continued. "I don't feel well. I can only eat fresh meat. If it is cooked I can't keep it down. The nightmares started the first night of the full moon." She looked at Elizabeth then, her eyes wide with horror. "You knew," she whispered.

Elizabeth shook her head, her eyes on Luke. "No."

"Then why did you send Sara in my place. It was so I wouldn't kill our guests, wasn't it?" Gemma's limbs began to shake, and her face grew even paler. "It didn't stop me," she cried. "I killed a girl. An innocent child. She was just a child. I tried to stop myself but I couldn't control the beast."

My god! It's not true. "You did not kill that girl, Gemma," Luke told her.

"I did, Uncle Luke." Gemma's voice broke, and Luke thought his heart would break. "I killed her as surely as if I had sunk my own teeth into her young flesh.

"No you didn't. And you didn't kill Green. And you didn't attack Sue."

"Sue. Oh my god! Is Sue all right? I don't remember attacking Sue."

Luke slammed his fist on the table so hard the dishes rattled, and both women jumped. "That's because you didn't attack Sue. I told you that. A man named David Woods killed those people."

Gemma licked her lips, and wiped her hands on her pants. Her eyes were wide with shock. "David?" That's the name of the man I met at the bar." She looked both relieved and determined. "Thank god I didn't actually kill anyone. But that doesn't change the fact that I am responsible for their deaths. I must have bit David that night. By our laws that means I must be put down."

Chapter Thirty Two

Jade ate three bowls of stew and almost an entire loaf of bread herself. As usual everything was cooked to perfection. She stopped herself just short of licking the bowl; after all it was almost spotless from the bread anyway. She patted her stomach. "Delicious as usual, Mrs G."

Mrs Grey beamed, and then she set about preparing a tray with two bowls and another loaf of bread. "Randy has a guest," she offered at Jade's questioning look.

Jade was pretty sure she knew who the guest was, and felt better knowing that Mrs G had a hand in taking care of her. She rose from the table."Thanks again, Mrs G," she said. "I have an appointment in town so I'll just get out of your way."

"Would you like me to call you a cab," Mrs G offered.

Jade barely concealed a shudder at the mere thought of getting into another one of those death traps. If she ever set foot in a cab in this town again it would be too soon for her. "Not this time, thanks."

After a quick shower, and changing into a clean shirt, and faded but comfortable jeans, Jade pulled on her hiking boots and took probably her last look around the room. She was really beginning to like this place. Too bad she probably wouldn't be coming back. She stuffed everything she owned into her pack, and left the room. In never paid to get too comfortable.

Ten minutes later a snowy white owl hopped between two dumpsters, and Jade stepped out. She fluffed her hair with her fingers, and then shook her head. *Get a hold on yourself girl. It's only an interview. It's not like anyone cares what you look like.*

Jade stepped into the dimly lit bar, and all eyes turned to her. It was a lot busier than the first time she'd been here. She spied an empty stool at the bar, and headed directly for it. She nodded at a few people, not surprised when they turned their heads away without acknowledging her presence, only to follow her with their eyes when she was past them. A few went so far as to move their chairs back when she drew near. By the time she reached the bar stool she felt like a pariah.

Moarté! The hated name echoed in her mind. *I'm only doing my job,* she thought mutinously. *Someone has to protect your sorry asses.* She didn't know why it bothered her so much this time, but it did. She should be used to being ostracized. She was the equivalent of judge, jury, and executioner. Death! *Moarté!*

She sat on the empty stool, now a good two feet away from the patrons on either side. She turned her attention to the bartender. "I'll have a beer, please."

The bartender wiped the counter in front of her. Then he stopped at the stool beside her. "Can I get you anything else," he asked ignoring Jade's presence.

So now I am invisible. Why am I so surprised? She wasn't sure why, but deep down she knew that Sue wouldn't have treated her so, even if she had known who she really was.

"Sure, Mike." The man's voice rattled with barely controlled fury, but the gorgeous smile never once faltered.

"You can get me another beer, and grab one for the lady while you're at it." He turned to Jade then, and offered his hand. "Hi. I'm Daniel. Daniel Dixon. You must be Miss Caer O'Connor from O'Connor Search and Rescue. I've been waiting for you."

At least he is friendly. And gorgeous. He wore an aura of power that was very becoming. *It has to be the wolf in him.* Jade glanced at the clock above the bar. She was five minutes early. "Have you been waiting long?"

"All my life." His voice was soft, sensual, and didn't do a thing for Jade, although she definitely enjoyed the eye candy. A couple of patrons guffawed. They may not want anything to do with Jade, but they were all very much interested in what Daniel might say to her. Daniel glared at them, and they quickly silenced. "Okay. You caught me. It has only been since I sent my first letter, nearly four years ago."

Jade winced. Had it really been four years since she had received the first letter from this man?

"Hey, don't sweat it. I understand people must apply for positions with your company all the time. I can't blame them. You have the best reputation around. That's why I was so persistent."

Jade visibly relaxed, and her natural smile made her face glow. "Shall we get right to business, or do you want to finish our drinks first."

Daniel looked around the room at all the wary, but too interested faces. "To tell the truth I'd rather do this somewhere else."

Jade didn't blame him. It couldn't be easy for him to be talking to the dreaded *Moarté* in front of his friends. Not to mention she was almost positive that he, and everyone else, had been ordered not to speak to her.

Jade took a swallow of the beer the bartender had finally placed before her. "Thanks, Mike," she called to his retreating back, as if he hadn't completely ignored her. She pulled a ten out of her pocket, and stuck it under her bottle.

"This one's on me." She indicated both hers and Daniel's beers, and slid gracefully off the tall stool. Waving her hand towards the door, she said, "Lead on McDuff."

They grabbed a corner booth at the greasy spoon at the corner. Jade didn't even glance at the menu when it came. "I'll have a hamburger, very rare, with the works, and a beer," she said.

"I'll have the same," Daniel said. "And could you add some fries to that?"

"No problem, Danny." When the waitress smiled at Jade it held real warmth. "Would you like fries as well Miss? We make them from fresh potatoes."

Her eyes are the color of a stormy sky, Jade thought. "No thank you."

She was rewarded with another sunny smile, and the waitress flounced off to place their orders.

"Danny?"

Daniel groaned. "I've known Missy since grade school. For some reason she refuses to acknowledge we aren't kids anymore."

"Well I for one like it. Makes you seem more approachable."

Daniel let out a low, rumbling laugh. "Is being approachable a prerequisite to the job?"

"It does help, sometimes. But a good nose and compassion are far more important."

The waitress returned with their food, and Daniel insisted on paying. He took a swig of beer, and Jade sensed more than saw, him eyeing her warily over the bottle. "A good nose?"

"That and a driver's license." She narrowed her eyes at him. "You do drive don't you?"

Once again, low rumbling laughter erupted. "Driver's. Pilot's. Do I get extra points for the pilot's license?"

Jade regarded him seriously. "Helicopter or plane?"

"Both. Helicopter and small plane. I don't have a commercial license. Mr Wulfson thought it would be a good idea if some of us could fly. He paid so we went."

A wave of desire washed over Jade at the mere mention of his name. Jade groaned inwardly. This was so not going to work.

Daniel took a bite of his hamburger. "You should eat your burger while it's hot. They're really good here."

They finished their meal in silence. The waitress cleared their plates, and brought them each another beer before Daniel finally broke the silence. "Listen, Miss Caer, I have to be honest with you."

"Honesty is good."

"I really want this job. If you give me a chance I know that I am the right person for this. I have been working for the Willow Bend Search and Rescue Team for eight years, and my recovery record is very good."

"That was in your letters -- All six of them." She smiled at him. He was so earnest. Her instincts had been right. He would be perfect for the job. It was too bad if his relationship with Wulfson was going to be a problem. "The company is based out of New York. We have a ranch at the bottom of the Catskills. We are often called to other countries so your passport needs to be current. Is that going to be a problem?"

Daniel shook his head, and Jade continued. "When we are not out in the field we live at the Ranch and help train the dogs. My Da ... Grandfather makes his living raising and training search and rescue dogs. He is getting along in years, but refuses to retire. You will get eight weeks vacation a year to start. We try to accommodate you for time, but that is not always possible." She mentioned a salary that was several times higher than Daniel had expected.

"When can I start?"

Jade smiled at his enthusiasm. *There are still a few things you need to know.*

Daniel sat back in his seat, positive he would pass the rest of the interview. "So inform me."

Daniel wasn't even aware that he had responded to an unspoken question. With a little work he would be able to communicate with her silently. "I came to town because your letter intrigued me. I'm offering the job because I like what I see."

"Thank you."

I take my privacy very seriously.

That is understandable.

Jade smiled. Their connection was strong, which was a very good thing. There were times when that connection could be the only thing to save their lives.

"There is one other question I need to ask before we settle this. Is there going to be a problem with Luke Wulfson if you work with me?"

Chapter Thirty Three

Jade knocked on the door, but didn't wait for an answer. She turned the handle and walked in, followed by Daniel Dixon. Luke didn't look surprised to see her there, or even to see Daniel with her. He just seemed broken.

"Hello Jade, Daniel." Luke inclined his head slightly. "Come in and have a seat."

"Are you here for me?" There was quiet acceptance in Gemma's voice.

"That depends on the answers I get here today." Jade replied.

They were standing in a large open room. There was a table set for three, with several extra chairs, at the end of the room that was obviously the kitchen area. There was a window over the sink, with the fridge and stove flanking the long counter. The other end of the room held a sofa, two chairs, a radio, no television that Jade could see, and one entire wall was a bookshelf. There were three windows at that end of the house. There were two closed doors which she presumed led to a bedroom, and a bathroom.

"I did it."

"Did what?" Jade watched the girl carefully for any signs of deceit.

"I need to be put down but Uncle Luke refuses to do it, and I'm not strong enough to do it myself."

Jade's heart melted at the sadness in the younger girl's eyes, but she stayed firm. "Why do you believe that you should be 'put down'?"

Gemma took a deep breath, her dark eyes tormented. "I am responsible for destroying the lives of at least four innocent people that I know of."

"Four?"

Gemma's voice broke. "I'm pretty sure I bit the man at the bar."

Oh you bit him alright. But he wasn't innocent. Not by a long shot. "Tell me why you bit him, Gemma? Did he do anything to you?"

"No. I don't know."

Jade's expression didn't change. She held Gemma's dark eyes with her own, glowing slightly with power. "You don't know. Or you won't say?"

Gemma struggled to break eye contact. Jade's own eyes flared slightly, and she held the girl steady.

"I can't," she whispered. "I don't remember."

Is she telling the truth, Daniel?

I have known Gemma for many years. I can't recall a time when she was ever dishonest.

I understand that she is a friend, and a pack member. I want you to disregard all that, and tell me whether you think she is lying at this moment.

Daniel saw the haunted expression in his friend's eyes, the trembling of her lip as she tried to hold back her sobs. She wasn't fidgeting. Her skin was not clammy. She didn't look anywhere except at Jade. She didn't look like anything other than a brave child, trying to own up to her mistakes. *No. Gemma is not lying.*

"Okay then." Jade glanced towards the two closed doors. "Elizabeth, is there a room we can use for privacy?"

"What are you..?" Luke stepped between Gemma and Jade.

Gemma placed her hand on her Uncle's arm, and gently moved him aside. "Please, Uncle Luke. Let us end this with some dignity."

That Luke wanted nothing more than to send Jade away, was evident in the way he glared at her. He shoved his hand through his hair, looked from Gemma to Jade, over to Elizabeth, and back to Jade, then he stepped aside.

Jade wanted to go. She wanted to go home, and hug Alicia, and Da, and Althea. She wanted to leave this child here, amongst the people who loved her, and let them sort this mess out. *She wanted to grab Luke and drag him somewhere they could be alone, and screw his brains out.* Jade shook her head to clear away the rampant thoughts. None of that was about to happen. She had a job to do.

Elizabeth indicated the closed door on the right. Gemma led the way into the bedroom. It was a comfortable room. A large skylight allowed the night stars to twinkle above them, and a cool breeze drifted in through an open window. A large bed was positioned directly under the skylight. Other than the bed, the only other furniture was a chair in front of a small vanity. The door to the closet was open.

Jade could see Luke through Daniel's eyes when she closed the door behind her. His face was thunderous. His eyes were so hopeless she wanted to cry when Daniel took up his position outside the door.

"Daniel." Jade couldn't help but hear the silent plea in Luke's voice.

"I am sorry, Alpha, but I cannot allow you to interfere."

Jade snapped the connection. She pushed the bed from the center of the room, and sat cross legged on the floor. She indicated the spot before her.

"Is this going to hurt," Gemma asked in a small voice.

"I hope not," Jade replied.

Gemma hesitated slightly before sitting on the floor facing Jade. Now that she was actually face to face with her judge and jury, Gemma was scared. Terror flared in her dark eyes. The only other indication of her fear was the nervous way she chewed on her bottom lip.

Jade reached across and took both of Gemma's ice cold hands in her own. "Close your eyes, Gemma. Take a deep breath. Now let it out very slowly, and think of the first time you saw David Woods."

The room was dark, and smoky. It was so crowded you could barely move. Gemma was with Luke's pretty secretary, Sara. She pointed across the room, and then dragged Gemma with her.

Gemma was sitting at the table with David Woods. Gemma was dancing with Sara. Gemma was at the table with David Woods again. She was drinking beer. She was happy. She had her wolf firmly under control.

Gemma rose, and left the table. She was almost across the room when she suddenly turned around, and looked at David across the room. He pulled a small package from his pocket, and dropped something into Gemma's glass.

The son of a bitch drugged her. No wonder Gemma lost control.

Gemma finished her business in the bathroom. She didn't realize that David had put something in her drink. She returned to the table and drank her beer. It tasted funny, and she wrinkled her nose, but she swallowed it. She watched Sara dancing with a man.

Gemma staggered out to the parking lot. She inhaled David's scent. He smelled like spicy muffins.

Gemma was on fire. Her body burned. The pain was unbearable. She was screaming. She bit down on the scream. Her canines sank into flesh. Everything was black.

How dare he? Not only did he drug the child, he raped her. The rage built until sparks flew from Jade's eyes.

Gemma's eyes popped open, and she screamed. The chair flew across the room, and slammed into the wall, landing in pieces on the floor. There was a scuffle outside the door. Energy flew from Jade, and the door lock slammed into place. *Stay out.* As quickly as it began, the scuffle ended.

What was wrong with her? If David Woods was alive, and standing in front of her at this moment, she had no doubt that she would rip him apart--again. Jade had to struggle to get herself under control. "It's okay, Gemma." She was hoping to sound calm, but the words came out in a growl. "I'm not going to hurt you."

"But?"

"It isn't your fault. None of it was your fault. You were drugged. David Woods drugged you. You were not under control of your actions when you sank your teeth into him."

"What about the bloodlust?"

Jade shook her head.

"I can only eat raw meat." Gemma was genuinely confused.

"That's because you are pregnant."

Gemma stared at Jade as if she had two heads. "What?"

"That bastard drugged you. And then he raped you. You are pregnant."

"Is that why you won't carry out my sentence? Because I am pregnant?

Jade sighed. "Gemma, listen to me very closely. You are not responsible for David Woods. His destruction was brought about by his own actions. He drugged you. Not the other way around. David Woods is responsible for his own death, and the deaths of the child in Toronto, and the man outside of town. David Woods is responsible for Sue. Not you."

Tears ran unchecked down Gemma's face. "I don't understand. I was there."

Jade wiped the tears from Gemma's face. "You saw what was happening through David's eyes, because you were connected to his wolf." Jade placed her hand on Gemma's abdomen, and closed her eyes for a moment. "You are carrying a life inside of you that you will be solely responsible for. It won't be easy for either one of you. Just be good to yourself and your son. Teach him to live by our laws, as well as those of man. I don't want to have to come back for either one of you."

Gemma sat in the middle of the floor, tears streaming down her face. Energy shimmered in the room, and the lock snapped open. *We will expect you in two weeks Daniel.* She had already planted the true location of the ranch deep in his subconscious where only he would ever find it, along with safeguards so he would never be able to pass on the information.

Jade flew out the open window.

Chapter Thirty Four

Two months.

It felt like a lifetime. A lifetime spent with half of her heart missing.

Jade folded the letter she had just read, and shoved it into the pocket of her jeans. Gemma was in Italy. Her parents were happily spoiling her. Everyone was counting the moments until the baby was born. *They're not the only ones.* Jade place her hand protectively over her own abdomen. *Only seven more months kids.* Seven months to go, and already her pants were growing snug.

Alicia ran past laughing, several pups nipping at her heels. *Come play with us.*

Jade smiled. "I have to feed the dogs first," she told her.

Alicia ran back, and grabbed the bag of food out of Jade's hands. Several nuggets fell out only to be snatched up by the tumbling pups. "Let me do that." Alicia narrowed her eyes at Jade, and tried to look stern. She failed miserably.

Jade laughed. Alicia shook her head, black curls flying, and dark eyes laughing. "You have to take it easy mommy. The babies."

Jade took the bag back from the child, dropped it on the ground, and pulled Alicia into her arms. "Are you happy, sweetheart?" Jade was. She could hardly believe how much life Alicia had brought to the ranch. Everybody adored her. She was growing stronger with each passing day, and the nightmares had almost stopped.

"Oh yes. I love you, and grandpapa, and Auntie Althea. When is Auntie Althea coming back anyway? We were going to make brownies today. Oh yea. I love Uncle Daniel, and I will love our babies." Alicia started giggling. "I think Uncle Daniel loves Auntie Althea too. I caught him making gaga eyes at her when she wasn't looking."

Jade laughed. Life was certainly good. If only Luke could be here it would be perfect. She forced the wayward thought from her mind, and made a point of looking around to see if they were alone. Then she leaned into her daughter and whispered. "Don't say anything, but I caught her making gaga at him last night."

The two of them laughed, the chores temporarily forgotten.

Later that night after tucking Alicia in and reading her a story, Jade took a cup of tea, and went out to sit on the porch swing. This was one of Jade's favourite times of day. Alicia was sleeping, Da was in bed, Daniel and Althea had gone for a run in the woods, and she was totally alone with her fantasies. The night was dark. Only a dim light showed through the window of the house, making the shadows dance along the porch rail. Jade relaxed, and her mind began to wander.

The smell of smoky pine tickled her nose, and her pulse quickened. It was amazing how a simple smell could make her body react. Luke appeared through the steam from her tea cup. His eyes were haunted, his face more gaunt than she remembered, and there was a small amount of gray in his hair. He looked so real. She could almost reach out and touch him.

"Mind if I sit?"

Jade sputtered, and the tea spilled. A hand snaked out, and snatched the cup from her shaking fingers. "Whoa. You don't want to burn yourself."

"What are you doing here?" Jade was stammering. She couldn't help it, and it made her angry. She couldn't believe he was really here.

"I couldn't stay away any longer." He stood on the edge of the deck looking across at her. "You left before I could thank you for Gemma."

"That's why you came? To thank me? I was only doing my job. You could have sent a letter." He was so the hottest male to ever walk the planet.

"If I sent a letter I couldn't do this." Luke crossed the deck, and gathered Jade into his arms. His lips, hot and strong, covered hers before she could blink.

She moaned as his tongue sought the moist heat of her mouth. It was a good thing he held her because her knees were jelly, and every bone in her body was melting.

"God I have missed you."

"What took you so long?" Jade slid her tongue between his lips for a little exploration of its own, while her hands slid under his shirt and caressed his bare skin.

"I had some business to tend to. Then I had to wait until the full moon had passed." He sat on the porch swing, and pulled Jade on his knee, sliding his hand beneath her sweater to caress her midriff. His hand slowly rose.

Her breath was coming in short quick pants. Why was he taking so long? She started unbuttoning his shirt. "Why wait until after the full moon. I like the full moon." Visions of them during their last full moon jumped into her head. She panted harder.

"I wanted you to realize this is us," he said. "It has nothing to do with the moon."

"Oh yes," she moaned as he gently thumbed one nipple. "This is definitely not the moon."

"I'm glad you see it my way."

Luke withdrew his hand from beneath her sweater, and Jade almost whimpered. When he lifted her, and set her on the porch swing she eyed him warily. When he knelt before her, and reached for her hand she laughed.

Luke growled at her. "Don't laugh. I'm serious."

Jade sputtered. "Sorry. Please continue."

Luke jumped up, and sat beside her on the swing. "Forget it. You ruined the mood."

Jade snuggled closer to him, snaking her arm around his waist and tucking herself beneath his arm. She looked up into his face, attempting to look contrite. "I'm sorry," she said. "Maybe I can restore the mood."

Luke leaned down, and captured her pouty lips, kissing her until her toes curled. When he finished, she looked up at him with passion glazed eyes.

"Forget it. I'm not asking. I'm taking charge. We are going to be wed as soon as possible. I can't live without you. You are my mate. Wolves do not let their mates go."

Jade sighed contentedly. She did so love a take charge kind of guy. Not that she had any intention of letting him have his way in everything, but it would be interesting watching him try. "That's good," she told him meekly. "The children will need a strong daddy to handle their mommy."

"Children?" Luke's expression was a mixture of horror and hope.

The story continues with ...
Blood Connection
Lynn Marie Simpson
ISBN: 978-0-9813539-2-0
www.pinelakebooks.ca

Do not move. They can't see you if you don't move.

The wind roared like a freight train barrelling down the tracks, straight for them. Alicia stared in horror as the massive ebony coach pulled by its two mammoth black bears burst through the clouds. *They can't see you if you do not move.* She prayed for divine intervention, even as she watched death coming for her.

The bears stopped, and snuffled the air. They couldn't find her. She was safe.

There was movement to her left. Terror gripped her throat, as little Megan ran straight for her. The bears turned as one, and sped straight toward the little girl.

Do not move. Do not move. Do not move. Even as the words ran through her mind, Alicia leapt toward the child.

She snatched the startled child into her arms, and stumbled, rolling as she fell to protect the child with her own body. Coming to a sudden stop, she sat up with the whimpering child tucked safely against her chest.

Thunder roared in her ears, as the bears' hot breath brushed her cheek. Megan whimpered. Alicia knew if they stayed were they were Megan would die. She couldn't live with the death of another innocent on her conscience.

There was a flicker of movement in her peripheral vision.

He stood there; Tall, Egyptian, and wearing only a loincloth that did nothing to hide his manhood. His tanned body rippled with muscles, and flames flickered in the golden sun tattooed on his broad chest. His eyes locked with hers, and she stopped breathing. Heat pooled at her center, and her blood ran hot. Alicia melted beneath the radiating heat of those golden orbs. He silently offered his hand.

Alicia's eyes flickered to the fluttering nostrils of the giant bear, and back to the nearly naked god.